NINE

Short Stories *of*
Passion, Betrayal
and Revenge

CHASE

THE

SUN

CHRISTINE SILK

CHARTWELL
PRESS

Chase the Sun: Nine Short Stories of Passion, Betrayal, and Revenge

Copyright © 2016 by Chartwell Press, LLC. All Rights Reserved.

For information about this title or to order other books and/or electronic media, contact the publisher:
Chartwell Press, LLC
12030 Sunrise Valley Drive, Suite 450
Reston, VA 20191
ChartwellPress.com
publisher@chartwellpress.com

Printed in the United States of America

Cover and Interior design: 1106 Design

Publisher's Cataloging-in-Publication Data
provided by Five Rainbows Services

Silk, Christine.
    Chase the sun : nine short stories of passion, betrayal, and revenge / Christine Silk.
        pages cm
    ISBN: 978-0-9963498-0-2 (pbk.)
    ISBN: 978-0-9963498-1-9 (e-book)
    1. Short stories, American. 2. Anthologies. 3. Literature—Collections. 4. Human behavior—Fiction. I. Title.
PS3619.I49 .C53 2015
813'.6—dc23
                        [LCCN]

TABLE OF CONTENTS

# CARICATURE

Wнo SAYS AN ARTIST can't have his moment, long after everyone thought his best days had passed? Oh, I'm not talking about an art-gallery show. I'm not talking about the *pièce de résistance* of one's life—although the caricature I drew that evening was a masterpiece, in its own peculiar way. It changed a poor creature's view of himself. Best of all, it put his obnoxious friends in their place. My drawing was revenge for their cruelty. It was the ultimate expression of my wicked sense of humor.

But, I'm getting ahead of myself. You can't understand what happened unless you understand *where* it happened. And where it happened was Le Vieux-Québec. Have you been there? If so, then you know that if you walk down the Rue du Trésor—which is really not a street, but a cobblestone alley—you will see the local artists selling their works. They prop their canvases against the old stone walls. For not much money, you can find decent drawings of Le Vieux-Québec, portraits of famous people, abstract creations in bright colors—the usual tourist art.

1

I used to have my spot on the Rue du Trésor, back when I made lithographs of Québec City landmarks. But life gets expensive with a wife and children, and now grandchildren. I found that I could make more money on weekend nights doing caricatures out by the gates of the Cathédrale Anglicane. I managed to get the spot when a friend pulled some strings with the city council. I told the council I'm an old man now, but a proud Québécois with many of my drawings of our beautiful city in the homes of tourists around the world. So how many more years will I have to set up my umbrella and easel? Not too many. Just enough to earn something for retirement.

I am only a stone's throw away from the Rue du Trésor. My new spot is less congested, but a lot of people still walk by. From under my umbrella, I can watch the slow-moving traffic circling the Place d'Armes, and the horses pulling calèches full of tourists. The Château Frontenac looms nearby, a massive Norman castle protecting the city. The castle contains tourists who are willing to pay hundreds of dollars a night for the privilege of staying at the best hotel in the city. When I was a child, I dreamed of staying there myself. I passed it on the way to church when my grandmother clutched my hand and pulled me through the streets, chiding me for walking so slowly. That's one of the reasons I started to draw. On paper, I was the master designer, completely in charge of my imaginary world. I could create anything: dragons at the Château's entrance, a lovely princess waving from the top tower, a knight on his horse galloping to rescue her. As a teenager, I designed a suite for myself in one of the corner towers overlooking the St. Lawrence River. I drew page after page of interior scenes, sometimes with people, sometimes not. It was my way of possessing, on paper, what I did not have in real life. It was all a childish dream, I know, but in the end, I came out with a skill that pays enough that I can put food on the table and a roof over my head.

Ah, but I'm getting distracted by the details of my past. The evening I want to tell you about happened during the summer. A warm breeze blew off the St. Lawrence River. Tourists and locals strolled the sidewalks while musicians serenaded them. Shops stayed open late. The air was heavy with the smell of grilled food and flowers.

It was a good night for business. People were in the mood to buy my art. Spectators had gathered around to watch me caricature my latest victim, usually a honeymooning couple or a family on vacation. Behind me, in the crowd, I heard some young men trying to persuade their friend to sit for me. I could tell they were Québécois.

"Come on, Jamie, let him do your picture," one said.

"Yeah, Jamie," another chimed in. "It'll be fun."

They were obviously drunk and out to have a good time. I hoped their friend would sit for me. I'd give them a good time, all right. If I played my cards cleverly, they'd all get a turn.

A caricature drawing is not a glamorous portrait. But it appeals to a basic instinct: many people want attention, even if it means that they are the butt of a joke. That is why they pay to have me draw them in funny poses, with their features exaggerated. I have a cruel sense of humor. Once, I drew an obnoxious girl in the pose of a fat, clumsy ballerina. Another time, I drew a vain, arrogant man as a pampered dandy, cautiously dipping his toe into the bathwater. The onlookers usually laugh as my drawing takes shape, and the person sitting in the chair squirms in anticipation, anxious to see how I have portrayed them.

When business is good, people elbow each other to give me their money, the next one thinking he'll fare better in my chair than the last one did. Tonight, these young men were no exception. They cajoled their friend to sit for me, bantering in English and French.

"Come on, Jamie," they said. "You're a good sport. Everybody's doing it." A jostle in the crowd, and they pushed Jamie toward me.

He hobbled forward, unsteady and disoriented, not sure where he should be. I guided him to the chair, sat in my own chair, and did my best to conceal my astonishment and horror. I had never seen a face as deformed as his.

One of his friends pressed money into my hand. Some of the onlookers stifled their laughter.

"Here's the twenty bucks," the friend said. He stepped back, snickering, and waited to see what I would do.

"Does he want his picture done?" I asked, turning to the one who had given me the money. "Because if not, I won't do it."

He shrugged. "Ask him."

I turned to the deformed creature who sat blinking beneath my light. "Well? Do you want me to draw you?"

"Yeah, yeah," he said, slurring the words with his deformed lips. "Do my picture."

I pocketed the money and sat down. I let the pen hover over the page while I appraised the face before me.

The horizontal center of his head, from ear to ear, was pushed in, so that his forehead and chin bulged forward, giving him the profile of a kidney bean. His small eyes seemed to move in and out of focus at random. His mouth was nothing more than a red slash beneath his caved-in nose. It stayed open a bit, exposing a tongue that worked back and forth behind small, crooked teeth. His skin was pleated with scar tissue—whether from surgery or the original deformity, I could not tell.

How to begin? I was accustomed to drawing the correct proportions that most faces have, and distorting them just enough to make a comical face. Should I draw this face and exaggerate it even more? Should I make this already wretched young man into a more repulsive object of sport for his snickering companions?

I was being asked to caricature a caricature.

I heard the bystanders murmur. Jamie's friends chuckled in anticipation.

I let my pen touch the paper.

When the eyes are confronted with disarray, they struggle to put it in order. So, I let the natural tendency of my eyes to seek order guide my hand. The misalignment of his face was corrected on my paper. The crooked eyes were straightened, the scarred skin smoothed, the pushed-in face pushed out.

The face that was being created on my easel was not handsome. It was, at best, average. But compared to the live model, the beauty was undeniable.

I could hear the whispers. One of his companions piped up. "Hey, that's no caricature."

"No?" I said, without looking up.

At this point, if I were working from a normal face, the onlookers would be talking and chuckling as my drawing took shape to poke fun at the model. But now there was a hush over the crowd—no laughter, no jesting, just the faint squeak of my pen on paper, and the din of the street life around us.

"Do you like sports?" I asked Jamie in my usual conversational tone.

"Yeah," he slurred. "I like hockey. And swimming."

I gave him the body of a swimmer. A bit too muscular, I admit, but what the hell. I drew under his feet a diving board, some water.

He fidgeted. I was almost done. My signature went in the lower corner. I turned my easel around so he could see it.

He bent forward and put his face close to the easel to study what I had drawn. He touched his own face, and then touched the drawing. I watched the expression on his face change: confusion, contemplation, and finally, recognition. The slash that was his mouth twisted into a smile.

I gently turned the easel back, tore off the paper, rolled it up, and gave it to him.

He immediately unrolled it and studied it again. Then he hopped off the chair and dashed clumsily toward his friends.

"This is me, this is really *me*," he said in his slurred speech, pointing at the drawing.

"Yeah, right, Jamie," one of them said. "Let's go get something to eat."

"This is what I look like," he insisted as they led him away. He held the drawing before him like a banner, walking more upright than before, almost prancing across the street. *"This is who I really am."*

I watched them walk away until they disappeared into the crowd.

I turned back to my easel and suddenly felt tired.

"Good night," I said to the lingering onlookers. "I am finished for today." I folded up my umbrella, packed my things, and went home.

CHASE
THE SUN

MY FRIEND RUTH CALLED to ask if I could do her a favor and escort a young boy to Miami. She told me he was her third cousin, or something like that.

I said sure. I live in Miami, so it was no problem to have a seven-year-old sit next to me on the airplane from Pittsburgh to Miami. I'd be doing the Frankfurt-to-Pittsburgh route earlier that day, and I'd have a six-hour layover—enough time to pick the kid up and bring him to the airport. Even if the kid turned out to be a brat, I could handle it for a few hours. In the four years I've been a flight attendant, I've learned how to deal with unruly kids.

His name was Luis and he lived in a rundown section of Pittsburgh where people took care of what they had, even though they didn't have much. Christmas lights in the windows were glowing brightly in the predawn gloom, and trash cans waited out at the curb for the trash trucks. My high heels crunched the snow as I walked up to the front porch. I wished I could have worn slacks, because my legs were freezing, but my flight-attendant uniform was the only thing clean enough to wear.

I almost slipped on a patch of ice on the creaky wooden stairs. I swore under my breath. By dinnertime, I wouldn't have to worry about ice or snow or cold legs. I'd be in Miami, in my sandals and bathing suit, sitting next to the pool, drinking margaritas, and polishing my nails.

I tried the doorbell. Broken. I knocked. A tall woman with dark hair opened the door. The house sighed a warm breath of fried egg and laundry soap into the frozen morning.

She stepped aside to let me in. I wiped the melted snow off of my eyelashes, careful not to smudge my makeup.

"Good morning. I'm Lisa Gonzalez, the flight attendant from North American Airlines," I said in Spanish, smiling and putting out my hand.

"I'm Felicia," she said in a brittle voice. She didn't bother to shake my hand. Another woman was sitting in a chair in the living room, sobbing and burying her face in her hands. Beside her stood a little boy, stroking her hair and murmuring.

He glanced at me, then turned his attention back to the crying woman.

"That's Luis," Felicia said. "And that's his mother. Her name's Sonia. She's my sister."

I've seen parents cry when they put their kids on a plane, but Sonia was almost hysterical, pleading with Luis and Felicia in Spanish.

I decided to act as if everything were all right. "It's nice to meet you, Luis," I said, talking louder than the woman's wailing. "And you, too, Sonia. We're going to have a great time. Why don't Luis and I get going. We have to make sure we get to the airport on time. The weather is getting bad."

"Let's go over here for a minute," Felicia said. "Luis is not ready yet."

I followed her through a doorway. In the dingy little kitchen, Felicia turned to me. "*Señorita,* listen. If it were up to me, I wouldn't let you walk out of the house with our little Luis."

I held up my hands and shrugged. "Well, don't let me do you any favors or anything. The only reason I'm here is because Ruth Diaz asked me to escort Luis to Miami. She's got bronchitis, so she couldn't do it herself. But if you don't want me to take him, no problem. The sooner I get going, the sooner I'll be home." I started for the door.

Felicia dropped the nasty attitude in one second flat. "I'm sorry. It's just that I'm worried about him."

"You don't trust me? I deal with kids all the time. I've got eight nieces and nephews myself."

Felicia shook her head. "It's not you I'm worried about. It's his father, Victor."

"Oh."

Felicia explained. "His father is entitled to visitation rights, even though he moved back to Colombia. That's what the judge says. So we're stuck here. Goddamn his soul straight to hell."

I couldn't tell whether this last comment was directed toward the judge or the father.

She went on. "I'd take Luis to California and let them try to find me. Victor doesn't even know where my mother lives in Los Angeles. I got lots of family there who'd kick Victor's ass so bad they'd have to take him out in a body bag. But my sister isn't strong. She's afraid to disobey the judge. She's afraid to move out of this house. She thinks if she even moves across town Victor will come back and really hurt her this time, even though I tell her we'd be safer in Los Angeles. But she won't listen to me." Felicia leaned closer and whispered: "He said Luis wasn't his when Sonia got pregnant. Didn't give her a dime. Gave her a good beating at least once a month, though, and she almost lost the baby. Now that Sonia doesn't want to go back with him, he's using the boy as a way to get revenge."

"So is Luis going or not?" I asked, looking at my watch. I wasn't being paid to be anyone's shrink, and I didn't really care about the family drama. "I should get going before it's too late for me to get out of this city." There was no use sticking around for all the details if the kid wasn't going. The plane wouldn't wait.

Felicia's anger changed to sorrow. "Me and Luis are the only ones in this family who are not afraid of Victor. *Mi niño* tries to be so strong. But he's only seven. He says he will be okay, for us not to worry."

I suddenly felt a twinge of guilt for being cold to her. She was only looking out for her nephew. I'd do the same thing if I were in her place.

I glanced at my watch. "Well, if we're going to catch that plane, we have to go."

I walked into the living room. Sonia started crying again when she saw me. She clutched her son and wailed: "Oh, *mi querido Luisito, no te vayas....*"

"Don't worry, Mama," he responded in English, wriggling out of her grasp. "I'll be okay. I'll be back right after the new year comes. I'll see what Christmas is like in Bogotá, and I'll draw you some pictures."

I couldn't help but notice how unenthusiastic he sounded.

"Bogotá?" I said. "I thought he was going to Miami."

"And from there, his father is taking him to Bogotá," Felicia explained. "He would've come here to get Luis, but there are people who are interested in him, if you know what I mean. I'm surprised Victor's even setting foot in Miami. He won't stay at the airport longer than he has to. Just long enough to get Luis onto the plane with him."

"Is he allowed to take the boy out of the country?" The last thing I wanted was to have my ass hauled before a judge for helping them violate a court order.

Felicia's face hardened again. "The lawyer was slick. He got the judge to agree to let Luis go to Bogotá." She paused. "Goddamn Victor and his lawyer."

I looked at the boy to see how he took Felicia's attitude toward his father, but his little face remained impassive, even resolute.

Luis grabbed his backpack and the handle of his rolling carry-on. He stood looking straight ahead, waiting.

The two women walked with us to the door. Sonia clutched Felicia's arm for support.

As we stepped outside into the freezing air, Felicia said to Luis, "If your father doesn't bring you back to Miami by January third, don't worry, I'll come right down to Bogotá to get you."

Sonia grabbed her son and hugged him, sobbing and murmuring that she loved him. Felicia peeled her sister off the boy. Then Felicia kneeled down and wrapped her arms around Luis. Her eyes were shut tight, but tears squeezed out. She whispered something to him, then let go.

"Don't worry, I'll take good care of him," I said, turning at the bottom of the porch stairs. The women said nothing. Luis followed me, letting the rolling bag bump down each stair.

The snow was falling hard. White flakes danced across our path as we sped down the highway in my rental car. The boy was silent the whole time, looking out the window. That was fine with me. I was too busy concentrating on the road to entertain him. I hoped the plane would be able to take off in these conditions. I didn't want to spend a minute more than I had to in this place.

My mind wandered to the Prada handbag and the five-inch Jimmy Choo peep-toe pumps I'd seen in *Cosmo* the other day. After all the hassles I'd put up with this week, I deserved to buy myself an early Christmas present.

The traffic was okay. We got to the airport with some time to spare.

I checked the departures monitor and saw that the storm had caused major delays and a lot of cancellations in Chicago. Storms like that moved from west to east. I'd be damned if I was going to spend the next few days snowed out in Pittsburgh when I could be sitting at the pool in Miami. If we could get on an earlier flight, we'd have a better chance of leaving on time.

I took his hand. "Come on, we have to go to the gate," I said.

We ran together. He kept up without complaining, pulling his bag behind him. We stopped long enough to get through security. Then we ran to the gate.

"Hello, Liz," I said to the round-faced woman behind the counter.

She smiled. "Hi Lisa. Working this flight today?"

"No. I'm escorting this young man to Miami." I gestured to Luis, who was standing beside me. "We're supposed to be on flight eleven twenty-five, but can you put us on eighty-three instead? The weather report looks bad, and we have to make the connection."

"Yeah, it's bad, all right, and the storm is headed our way. O'Hare just closed. We're bracing ourselves for major delays." Liz picked up the phone. "They're getting ready to shut the door on eighty-three, but I'll tell them to wait. I'll just need to see IDs for the two of you."

"Liz, you're an angel," I said. "Next time you're in Miami, dinner is on me."

"You got it," she said, smiling and checking our IDs. She typed some information into her computer and gave us the thumbs up.

I grabbed Luis's hand and ran.

Five minutes later, we were in our seats.

"Do you think we might not be able to go?" he asked almost hopefully, his face pressed against the window, watching the snow.

"I think we'll be able to take off," I said.

Luis was staring out the window at the bundled-up men loading the luggage onto the plane. They were bulky and slow in their heavy winter clothes.

"See how they're dressed?" I said. "When we land in Miami, all the baggage guys will be in shorts. That's what I love about flying. You can chase the sun anywhere, and never be stuck in bad weather if you don't want to be."

"Do you fly all the time?" Luis asked.

"Several times a week. I'm a flight attendant."

"You look like one."

"I do?"

"Yeah. You're tall and pretty," he explained. "That's how they are on TV."

"Ooh," said a woman's voice hovering over us, "that boy is a darling. You'd better keep him, Lisa honey. Is he one of your nephews?"

I looked up at the flight attendant who was standing nearby—an old friend of mine.

"Hello, Shawna," I said. "This is Luis. He's Ruth's cousin. I'm escorting him to Miami, and then he's going to Bogotá for Christmas. Ruth would have done it herself, but she's in bed with bronchitis."

"Poor Ruth," Shawna said. "You working this weekend?"

"Nope. I'm off till Thursday. I'll be at the pool with Marty until then."

"Marty? Have you told me about him?"

I smiled. "I don't know. But he's really cute, and he gave me a Dior bracelet for my twenty-fifth birthday."

"Sounds serious. Is it?"

I shrugged. "Depends on what he gives me for Christmas."

She chuckled. "Ain't that the truth. You can't let these men take you for granted."

The pilot announced the plane was ready for takeoff. I flipped through a magazine. Luis watched Shawna do the safety demonstration. Then he eagerly looked out the window as the plane took off. To him, it was all new and exciting. To me, it was the same old routine.

White flakes blurred past the window as we accelerated. The sky was an opaque ocean of gray and white. After a few minutes of steep climbing, we broke through the snowy clouds.

Luis pointed at the pale winter sun. "Look, there's the sun, Lisa! I've never been above the clouds before."

"Cool, isn't it?"

"Yeah, really cool," he agreed, gazing out the window.

Shawna came over. "Here, Luis honey, I have cookies and a deck of cards for you. There's also a box of crayons and some paper. Let me know if you need anything else."

"Thank you," Luis said, eagerly taking the items.

The flight was quiet and uneventful. No turbulence, no screaming babies. Luis kept himself occupied. He always said please and thank you when something was offered to him. Most of the time, his face was turned toward the window. I noticed that his black hair was neatly cut. His jacket was threadbare around the collar, but it was clean.

I decided I liked him. Not that I wanted to have kids or anything, not for a long time. My sisters used to be in shape like me, but now that they have kids, they're all carrying twenty extra pounds, and they don't even keep up their manicures.

Luis drew pictures of cars and trucks with his crayons, making sure to put each crayon back in the box as he finished with it.

"Do you like cars?" I asked.

"Yes. When I'm older, I want to have a Ferrari," he declared.

"They're expensive."

"That's okay. I'll work hard and save my money. I already saved seventy-eight dollars shoveling snow for my neighbors and selling candy."

"Do you keep it in a piggy bank?"

"No. Aunt Felicia keeps it for me. She says piggy banks aren't the best place. People break them."

"Oh. You mean you broke it by accident?"

"No. My father did. On purpose. He did it when I was five. He was looking for money to buy drugs. That's what Aunt Felicia said."

"Sounds like your father is not on Aunt Felicia's favorite-people list. Do you remember it happening?" I asked.

"I remember the broken bank. The money was gone. So was my father." He said this without emotion, and continued to color the truck wheels black.

"When was the last time you saw your father?"

"When I was six. He came over in the summer. My mom cried a lot."

"Oh. How come?"

"She was upset at him. I think he hit her a few times."

"Did he hit you too?" I was starting to sound like one of those TV lawyers. At any rate, I'd have something interesting to tell Marty when we were sitting around the pool.

"I don't think so. He did lock me in a closet, though."

"Really?"

"Yeah. Because I spilled some milk when I was pouring it in my cereal. He got mad. He told me to get in the closet. Then he locked it."

I was starting to get a headache. I rubbed my forehead.

"He forgot about me," Luis said quietly, looking down.

"What?" I wasn't sure I heard him right.

"He forgot about me. In the closet."

"How do you know he forgot about you?"

"I heard him leave. Then Aunt Felicia got me out when she came home from work. I was very thirsty. And hungry. It was hot in there."

He looked at me. His dark eyes were wide.

"Did your dad apologize?" I asked. Like it would make a difference.

Luis shook his head. "He said the door wasn't really locked. He said I could've gotten out if I wanted to. But I tried and it was stuck. Aunt Felicia had to open it for me." Suddenly, he asked: "Do *you* think my dad lied to me, about the door being locked? Aunt Felicia says he lied."

He waited for my answer.

"I … I don't know your father at all," I stammered, "so I can't say whether he was lying."

He sensed my evasion. The vulnerability in his eyes disappeared behind a veil of indifference.

"Yeah, right. It doesn't matter anyway," he said.

Just then, breakfast was served. He sat up straight, eager to see what it was.

We ate in silence. I thought about what he had told me, wishing … what? I wished he wouldn't tell me his family problems. I had enough problems of my own. The world sucks and I can't save it.

In a few hours, we'd be landing, and I would find Mr. Victor Gomez, give him his son, and go home to my condo. My job would be over. What he did with his kid was his business.

I'd be with Marty at the pool, having fun and forgetting all about today.

Luis finished eating and lay back in his seat, paging through a comic book.

I'm going to deliver this little boy to a man who thought nothing of locking him in a closet, alone, all day, without food or water. A man who punched his mother when this little boy was still just a baby inside her tummy. The thought popped into my head from nowhere.

I was starting to sound like Aunt Felicia. I reminded myself none of this was my problem. The kid had a right to see his father. That's what the judge ordered.

I looked at my watch. Less than two hours from now, my responsibility for this little boy would be over.

Luis tapped me on the arm.

"I'm thirsty," he said.

"I'll get you a drink."

I came back with apple juice.

"Thank you," he said.

"You're welcome. Are you doing anything special for Christmas? A special dinner or something?"

Luis shrugged. "Depends. My father doesn't like to cook."

"What kind of toys do you want for Christmas?"

Another shrug. "Nothing. My father says he doesn't have any money for presents. But that's okay. I'll make him a drawing and give him that. He likes trucks. I'll draw him a truck." Luis got to work on a blank sheet of paper. Then he interrupted his drawing, searched his backpack, and handed me a picture.

"That's my father," said Luis.

I looked at the snapshot. Victor was wearing a wife-beater. His beefy arms encircled Luis, who looked about four or five

in the picture. Luis was straining against those tattooed fore-
arms, as if he wanted to wriggle away, but he'd managed to
smile bravely for the camera.

There was something about Victor's face I didn't like.
I studied the picture again. His mouth was cruel.

I knew the type. Victor Gomez was exactly the kind of
passenger I hated dealing with. I could tell when they'd done
jail time. They didn't have much: maybe a dirty duffel bag
and a one-way ticket. They acted polite, but they harassed
you. Always checking you out, asking for a million little
things. More peanuts. Another drink. A napkin. *Headset is
broken; can I have another one? Hey, ya know, you're kinda pretty. You
remind me of that actress, I forget her name.* Then they'd ask you
for a date and wouldn't take no for an answer. Sometimes
they'd wait for you when you got off the plane and they'd
try to follow you.

One of them followed my friend Paula to her apartment.
I don't like to think about what happened to her.

I gave the photo back to Luis.

No money to give his son a present.

Couldn't the man just scrape together a few dollars to give
the kid something? A toy car or a coloring book, for God's
sake? They don't cost much.

I can't afford to worry about it, I reminded myself. I had
a tropical weekend to look forward to. It wouldn't be fair to
Marty if I were distracted about something that wasn't my
problem.

I kept quiet for about a minute. But something wasn't
right, and it bothered me. I let myself ask the question. "Do
you want to be with your father for Christmas?"

He turned his dark eyes on me and appraised me. He looked wise for a seven-year-old, deliberating how he should answer.

"The judge said I should go. My father has rights, too."

"But what do *you* want?"

"I want to help my mother. She needs me to help her."

"But do you *want* to be with your father? Do you *like* him?"

It was in his eyes just a fleeting second—not the kind of look you'd expect to see in a boy who truly loved his father, who wanted to see him and spend Christmas with him.

"He is my father. I should love him." Luis sounded as if he'd heard it a million times. "My mother will miss me. So will Aunt Felicia. And I like the snow. But next year it will be there again when Christmas comes." His bottom lip quivered, but he held himself together. Brave little soldier, carrying out his duties. Doing what the adults tell him to do.

What more could I say? I leaned back and closed my eyes, trying not to think about anything. The next thing I knew, Shawna was gently nudging me. "C'mon honey, you have to put your seat up. We're landing soon."

I looked next to me. Luis was curled up, asleep. His long eyelashes were dark against his baby-smooth cheeks.

We taxied to the gate. I waited until everyone had exited. Shawna came over.

"Are you going home now?" she asked.

"Not yet," I said. "We're early. I'll take him to the staff lounge until we can meet up with his father."

"I'll see you there then," Shawna said. "I have to wait around for the Dallas flight."

Luis woke up and rubbed his eyes. "Is my father here?" There was fear in his voice. Or was I imagining that?

"Not yet," I said. "We're early."

I helped him get his luggage, and we left the plane. The staff lounge was empty. Luis sat on a chair, still groggy.

"Why don't you sleep a little more," I said. "It'll be awhile before I take you to your father. He isn't expecting you yet."

Shawna came running into the lounge. "There's been a plane crash in Pittsburgh!" Her eyes were wide with shock.

"What?"

She turned on the television. "Look! It's on the news!"

Sure enough, there was footage of the burning airplane in a field. The cause of the accident was undetermined, but several people on the flight had already died from smoke and flames.

Other flight attendants came in to see the news. They were all talking and shaking their heads in disbelief.

"I was supposed to have been on that flight," I said to nobody in particular. "I was almost killed."

Luis heard me, and his face was pale. "That means I would've been killed, too. My mom's going to be so worried. So is Aunt Felicia." His voice started getting hysterical. "We have to call them. Call them, Lisa! Tell them we're okay!" He tried to hold back his tears.

I put my arm around him. "Hold on, Luis. I'll call them in a minute. Let's just pull ourselves together, okay? We're safe."

"Yeah," he said, rubbing his eyes to keep the tears away, "but I don't want them to be worried."

I didn't hear the rest of what he was saying. My mind was racing, making all kinds of crazy plans, thinking of a way out.

"Listen, Luis, I have to go check something, okay? You stay here. Shawna will take care of you till I get back." The television screen switched to a commercial for margarine. "Shawna, can you stay here with Luis? I'll be back soon."

"Sure, honey, I'll watch him." She patted a spot next to her on the sofa. "Come on over here, Luis honey. You can sit next to me, and we'll watch TV and eat a muffin, okay? Everything's gonna be all right, sweetheart. I'll get you some juice."

"I'm not hungry," he said, not moving. His eyes were round with fear. "My dad will be here soon."

I kneeled down and hugged him. "Don't worry, Luis. I'll be right back. Trust me. Go sit with Shawna. She'll help you."

He clutched his backpack to his chest and went to sit next to her. Shawna put her arm around him and said something that made him smile.

I put on my blue blazer, with the logo pin of the airlines on the breast pocket. I took off the name tag and put it in my purse. I left my purse in the lounge and walked out into the terminal. I looked like an airline representative now, not just an ordinary flight attendant.

I walked through the crowd. Things were beginning to get chaotic as the news spread about the accident and the bad weather. I could see a lot of worried faces. People gathered around television screens in the waiting areas, trying to find out what was happening.

It took me about fifteen minutes to find him, but there he was, off to the side, chewing gum and looking as if he needed a cigarette. He wore a black t-shirt. His hair was combed back. The mouth was cruel, just like in the picture.

"Mr. Gomez?"

"Who are you?" he demanded. He looked like he was trying to disguise himself with the sunglasses and a new goatee so his enemies wouldn't recognize him.

"I'm from North American Airlines. My name's Lidia Perez," I lied. "I understand you were waiting for your son? Luis?"

His mouth tightened. "Who wants to know?"

I switched to Spanish. "Look, Mr. Gomez, I don't know if you heard, but flight eleven twenty-five crashed and burned. It doesn't look as if there are many survivors." I paused, trembling inside. "Your son was on that flight."

I started to cry, in a professional way.

His demeanor changed. He took off his sunglasses, and gave me a hard stare, as if I was somehow to blame.

"I ... I'm sorry," I stammered. "This incident is hard for all of us. I lost some friends on that flight. People I work with."

He appraised me shrewdly. I was afraid. I bought time and avoided his stare by dabbing my eyes with a tissue I found in the pocket of the jacket, and tried to pull myself together.

After a while, he spoke. "How much money will there be?"

"Excuse me?"

"Insurance money. How much? You airlines always pay the survivors."

"That will be determined by the courts, after they find out what caused the crash. If there's a class-action lawsuit, you'll have to file a claim and go to court."

I didn't know if this was true, but it sounded good.

He shifted his feet, and looked uncomfortable. Maybe Felicia was right. Maybe he was wanted by too many people and wouldn't dare set foot in court.

"Will his mother get anything? We're divorced."

"It depends. The cause of the crash has to be determined first. It takes a long time." Son of a bitch. How could he think of money when I was trying to tell him his son was dead? "I am so sorry, Mr. Gomez. You must be devastated by this news."

I felt as if I were reminding a fellow actor of his lines. On cue, he rearranged his face into a look of grief. But his mouth remained hard and his eyes were cold.

"Yeah, I'm really broken up about it. That kid was my son."

"I am so sorry," I said, and reached out to touch his arm, just to prove that I meant what I said. He jumped back as if I had burned him with a cigarette, and then he looked at me. His lips peeled back in a smile.

"Hey, I appreciate it." He grabbed my arm, and his grip was like iron. "Why don't we go over to that bar and talk about it? You tell me about your friends, I'll tell you about my boy. It'll be good for both of us."

We started walking. He kept his tight grip on my arm. It made my skin crawl.

"I really need your help with making the claim," he said. "I can't stay here in Miami. So I want you to get the settlement for me, okay? It's the least you can do for me, given that your airline killed my son. I'll give you half, okay? What's your name again?"

"Lidia," I said. "Lidia Perez." I smiled. "I would love to spend time with you, Mr. Gomez. But I have to talk with other passengers right now." I tested him. "How about if I meet you later—say, in three hours? Then we can talk."

He frowned and scanned the room. "No. I can't. I have a plane to catch. You ever get to Bogotá?"

I nodded.

"Then let's get together there," he said. It sounded more like a command than a request.

I smiled my charming smile again. "I would love to, Mr. Gomez."

"I'm serious, Lidia. You come to Bogotá and find me." He let go of my arm to write something on a crushed cigarette pack. "Here's my phone number." He handed it to me. I took it as if it were a jewel.

"Now how about yours," he insisted.

"Okay." I wrote down a fake number on a parking slip. Area code 212.

"And your address while you're at it."

"Sure," I said, pretending to be flattered. I made up some address and gave it to him.

He read it. "I get to New York every so often. I'll look you up."

"You do that, Mr. Gomez," I said. "Goodbye."

He watched me walk away. I felt as if his eyes were burning holes through my clothes.

When I returned to the lounge, Shawna was sitting on the sofa, talking to Luis. I threw Victor's phone number in the garbage.

I was jumpy and paranoid. Suppose Victor followed me here and was waiting outside the door? If he found out I had lied to him ... I forced myself not to think about it.

"Everything okay?" Shawna asked. "You look like you just saw a ghost."

"I'm okay," I said. "Come on, Luis, we have to get you ready for the next plane."

Luis rose heavily to his feet. He looked exhausted and unhappy.

"My father is here, right? To take me to Bogotá?"

I ignored his question. "We don't have much time. Hurry," I urged him.

"Did you call my mom and Aunt Felicia?"

"Not yet. But I will. I promise."

"They'll be worried," he said. "My mom won't stop crying. Even after you call her."

"Let's get to the plane first."

We took a back stairway to the lower level. He had a bewildered and fearful look in his eyes, but he didn't say a word. I maneuvered him through the crowds to the United terminal. The line at the counter wasn't too long. I kept a lookout for Victor.

"Two tickets on the next flight to Los Angeles," I said.

The ticket agent punched up the information on the computer screen. "That'll be flight twenty-two sixty-seven at gate thirty. The best fare I can give you is twelve hundred per ticket, first class. It's all that's available."

"Okay," I said, handing him the credit card. I wasn't going to worry about money right now. The Prada handbag and Jimmy Choo shoes would have to wait.

Luis interrupted my thoughts. "Why are we going to Los Angeles? What happened to my father?" he demanded.

I ignored him and scanned the crowds as we made our way

to the plane. He kept pestering me with questions. "When are we going to call my mother and Aunt Felicia? Why can't we just call them now?"

"I'll tell you everything soon."

In the lounge near our departure gate, I sat him down in a chair facing the windows. I stood in front of him, my back to the window, so that I could watch who was coming and going through the terminal.

"Luis, let me explain. I'm taking you to Los Angeles, where your grandmother lives. Would you like that better than seeing your father?"

"See my grandma? Not my father?" He wrung his hands and choked back tears. "My father will be really mad if I don't see him. He'll come after me and my mom and Aunt Felicia. He said he would. He said he'd kill us if we didn't do what the judge said. I don't want him to hurt my mom anymore. Take me to see him so he'll leave my mom alone." He started to sob and rub his eyes with his fists.

I put my hands on his shoulders. "Luis, it's okay. Your father won't come after you. I promise. Do you really want to spend Christmas with your father?" If the boy really wanted to be with his dad, I could undo the lie by sending Luis to his father with a plausible excuse: "Oops, Mr. Gomez, good news. Your son was on a different flight after all. The computers got it wrong."

Luis sniffled and wiped his nose with his sleeve.

"If you want to go see your grandmother, we have to get on the plane now," I said.

"My father really won't hurt us? He won't come after us?"

"Really. I promise. He won't even know where you are. Felicia said he doesn't know where your grandmother lives. She said you have a bunch of uncles in Los Angeles who will …" I was going to say "kick his ass so bad he'll end up in a body bag," to use Aunt Felicia's phrase, but I decided to make it more gentle. "You have a bunch of strong uncles and cousins who love you very much and will protect you. They won't let your father anywhere near you."

Luis appraised me to see whether I was telling the truth. I held his gaze. I had never felt more truthful in my life.

"He won't know I'm there?" Luis asked again. "And he won't know if my mom is there, too?"

"Not unless you tell him. I sure as hell won't." I scanned the room to be sure Victor Gomez wasn't lurking somewhere in the crowd.

Luis took a deep breath. "I'll go to my grandmother's. Please tell my mom and Aunt Felicia I want them there, too."

"I will. I promise."

We boarded the plane. Luis was at the window seat. I walked the entire length of the cabin twice, including first class, and checked out each passenger to be sure there were no familiar faces.

Luis kept his gaze focused out the window. The Miami sky had turned cloudy, and big drops of rain pelted the glass.

"It never snows here, does it?" he asked.

"Never."

The plane sped down the runway. I didn't start to relax until the wheels were off the ground.

"Look at the clouds," Luis said. He pointed out the window as the plane ascended. "We're going to fly right into them. Just like we did in Pittsburgh." A minute later we broke through the storm clouds. "Look," he said. "The sun is shining on us now. We must be really high up." He turned to me and smiled the first real smile I'd seen on his young face. "We're really chasing the sun today, aren't we, Lisa?"

I smiled and squeezed his arm. "Yes, Luis, we're chasing the sun."

3   ENSENADA

KOREY ROBERTS HAD BEEN dreading this moment for months. As he sat in the Lido Grille, sipping his coffee, his wife Tiffany sat across from him, paging through a tour guide.

"It says there's great shopping here," Tiffany said, pointing to a page. "One of the stores has amazing deals on turquoise jewelry. Another one has fifty percent off on opals and emeralds."

They were on the uppermost deck of the *Sol del Mar*, a large cruise ship that specialized in tours between Los Angeles and Cabo San Lucas, with ports of call in between. Korey sat at a breakfast table that was right next to a glass wall with a view of the entire port town of Ensenada, Mexico. It was a pretty setting, with the mountains surrounding the little town. Small stucco houses dotted the green hillsides and became more crowded together as they reached the shore.

Korey peered out the window to the dock ten decks below. There, in the shadow of the cruise ship, Korey saw

Mexican women dancing for the passengers who had begun to disembark. The dancers' bright, flouncy skirts fluttered like birds' wings to the rhythm of the guitars strummed by men in traditional sombreros and embroidered jackets. It all looked so inviting. But Korey was terrified, and he calculated which excuse would be most likely to persuade Tiffany to stay on board.

She drank the rest of her orange juice and pushed her half-eaten omelet away. Korey had eaten only a bite of a sweet roll, but Tiffany was too distracted to notice.

"Let's grab an apple and get going," she said. Her hair and makeup were already in place, and she was wearing a turquoise-and-canary-yellow outfit that showed off her narrow hips, thin legs, and well-endowed chest. Days spent sunbathing next to the pool on Deck 9 had turned her already-tan complexion an even deeper shade of brown. Her gold necklaces and dangly earrings glimmered, and her long black hair fell straight down to her waist. If Korey's stomach hadn't been in knots, he'd have been more than happy to take his bride wherever she wanted to go. But there was no way he was going to leave the ship.

"I think we should stay on board," Korey ventured. "We've already been to three other Mexican ports. What'll we see here that we haven't seen before?"

Tiffany stood up. "Baloney. We paid good money for this cruise, and I want to see everything. Even Encinitas."

"Ensenada," Korey corrected her.

"Whatever. It looks like an adorable little place."

"It'll be just as grimy as Mazatlán," Korey pointed out.

"How do you know? Have you been here before?"

Korey didn't answer. He followed her out of the Lido Grille to the elevators.

"Let me just grab a few things from the cabin, and then we're good to go," Tiffany said.

Korey walked behind her, and when they got to the cabin, he collapsed onto the bed and closed his eyes.

After a few minutes, Tiffany announced: "Okay, I'm ready."

Korey didn't stir. "Why don't you go without me," he said. "I don't feel so hot."

Tiffany pulled his arm. "Come on, Korey. You've been fine this whole trip, and now all of a sudden you're sick? I don't buy it. You just drank too much at dinner last night, that's all. Some fresh air and sun will do you some good."

"You're right. I'll just go up to the pool and read for awhile."

"No way. Let's go ashore. I promise we won't spend the whole day there. We'll just look around a little, check out those jewelry stores, and then come back here to the ship for dinner. Okay?"

Korey grunted.

"Come on, Korey. I wanted to do an actual bus tour, but you hate buses. I wanted to have dinner at this seafood place in the middle of the town I read about, but I'm willing to give that up, too. You have to meet me halfway. Come on." She tugged on his arm, and her bracelets jingled.

Korey opened his eyes and smiled up at his bride. "You Filipina women are persistent little monkeys, aren't you?"

Tiffany smiled. "That's right. And you white fish can be such a drag."

Since the day she met him, she'd teased him about looking like a fish because his mouth was exceptionally wide, his lips were full, and his skin was white like the underbelly of a fish (although he had managed to acquire a faint ruddiness from sunbathing during the last week). His whole face, in fact, had a peculiar horizontal orientation, as if it had been stretched sideways. But for this strange proportion, he could almost have been considered good-looking. He was tall. Tiffany had told him on her first date that she wanted to marry a man who was a foot taller than she was and knew how to mix a perfect mai tai. "I'm your man, then," he had told her.

Tiffany gave his arm another tug. "You won't regret it, Korey, I promise. After dinner, I'll make it all up to you." She gave him a knowing wink.

Korey tugged on her arm, trying to pull her down onto the bed. "How about right now?"

"No. Later. Now let's go."

KOREY KEPT A SHARP LOOKOUT as they disembarked the ship. What he was looking for, he couldn't say. Just something out of the ordinary, something that would warn him of danger. He tried not to compare the way everything looked now to the way it had looked then, seventeen years ago, when he had last been here. He'd thought he'd never see this place again, and yet, here he was. He shivered, despite the warm air and sunshine, and pushed his sunglasses firmly into place under his wide-brimmed hat.

"Hey, *Señor,* I take picture," a man with a camera said, jumping in front of them as they walked.

"No, that's okay," Korey said, walking faster around the man.

Tiffany put her hand on her husband's arm. "Let's just have him take our picture, Korey. It can't hurt."

"It's a waste of time, and I don't want to do it," Korey argued. "Plus he wants money."

"Well, *I* want our picture taken," Tiffany pouted. "We don't have to buy it if it's no good."

Korey stood there, reluctantly. Her willfulness, which could be amusing, was beginning to irritate him.

The man with the camera said: "Señor, take off hat and glasses?"

"No, I'll leave them on," Korey said.

"Oh, just take them off," Tiffany said, swiping his hat off his head. "We're in the shade."

Korey left his sunglasses on and didn't smile for the camera. After the pictures were taken, Tiffany kissed him on the cheek.

"You're such a grouch today. Let's get you something to drink to put you in a better mood."

Korey put his hat back on, looking around yet again for anything out of the ordinary.

A sweaty, fat man in a straw hat walked up to them. "I have taxi. I take you around. To nice place."

"No, thank you," Korey said, pulling his wife away.

"We just want to get some fruit juice," Tiffany said.

"Agua fresca at Hector's, two mile that way," the fat man said, pointing. "I take you."

"No, thanks," Korey said, pulling Tiffany's arm harder.

Tiffany wriggled away from her husband and stood there, glaring at him. "What is up with you? You're acting like a total jerk."

"I'm sick of being hustled. I don't like Mexico and I just want to leave."

"You said you loved Cabo."

"I do love Cabo. I don't love Ensenada."

"Have you ever been here before?" she asked.

"Once. When I was nineteen."

"Oh, you never told me about that," she laughed. "Was it with some girlfriend?"

"No, it was with my family, on a cruise like this one. Nothing to report. Except that it's a shitty little town, it made me sick, and I really want to go back to the ship and just read and swim."

"Oh, stop being such a grouch," Tiffany said. She started walking and then stopped and pointed. "See that taxi over there? Why don't we hire it."

"I don't feel comfortable...." Korey began. The taxi driver, a slender man who looked like he was in his late-twenties, was leaning against his car, text messaging on his cell phone. He wasn't paying the slightest attention to his surroundings.

Korey stopped midsentence. He knew his wife would only persist in looking for a taxi driver. Better to choose one himself, one who looked safe, than to let her choose—or worse yet, to let a driver choose them.

"Okay, he looks fine," Korey said.

Tiffany went up to him. "Excuse me. Can you take us around?"

The man held up a finger, telling her to wait until he'd finished texting. After ten seconds, he slipped his phone into his pocket and said in good English: "Where to?"

"Oh, how about to the best agua fresca place in town?" Tiffany said. "Then let's hit the jewelry stores. My husband promised me a new bracelet for our three-month anniversary." She laughed.

Korey sat in the back seat of the taxi, glumly staring out the window, his hat and sunglasses firmly in place. Tiffany sat in front with the driver, chattering with him and laughing. Korey could tell that by the end of the day, the taxi driver would be her new best friend, and she'd reward him with a big tip if he didn't do anything stupid to piss her off.

Out the window, Korey saw children begging tourists for coins. One of the girls was a five- or six-year-old with a dirty brown face, straight black hair, and ragged clothes. Seeing her brought up a memory he wanted to forget. Street trash, he reminded himself.

"Is there still a place called Ponte Duarte around here?" Korey asked, cutting in on the conversation. He had interrupted his wife in the middle of her story about what kinds of daiquiris they'd sampled in Cabo San Lucas, but she didn't seem to mind.

"Yes, there is," the taxi driver said, keeping his eyes on the road.

"Why do you ask, darling?" Tiffany said, pleased that he was finally beginning to participate. "Do you want to go see it?"

"No," Korey said. "I read about it in a tour book somewhere, and I was just wondering."

"It's a cove," the driver said. "A popular place for those who know about it."

"Is it haunted or something?" Korey asked.

"What in the world makes you ask *that* question?" Tiffany said. "You always get on my case about going to a psychic."

"I heard it has some legends attached to it," Korey said. "I heard it's a place where people have been lost or killed. At least, that's what the tour book said."

The driver looked at him curiously in the rear-view mirror, but Korey pretended not to notice. Korey regretted saying anything. He'd already said too much, and he was exposing himself unnecessarily.

"Sometimes the ocean currents sweep things there, including bodies," the driver said. "Two or three times that I can remember, victims have been discovered."

"Really," Korey said, his throat dry. "Hey, Tiffany, I could use a bottle of water."

Tiffany dug around in her purse. "Would you like some water, too, Eduardo?" she asked the driver.

"No, thank you," he said, holding up his own plastic bottle.

"Listen, Korey," Tiffany said, "Eduardo was telling me about another jewelry store farther out that has even better deals than the other stores I told you about. How about we go check it out, then grab some lunch? I love Mexican food, you know."

"You like chimichangas?" Eduardo asked.

"I love them!" Tiffany said.

"There's a little place you should try, owned by my friend. I know, I know, all the taxi drivers will tell you that. But this is the real deal. The place is small, and it's authentic. Only the locals go there, no tourists."

"Sounds great!" Tiffany said.

"We can't go there," Korey said. "We don't know what kind of illness we'll get."

"Can I tell you something?" Eduardo said. "My friend was trained as a cook in San Diego. He used to work for one of the resorts there. His standards are even better than most American-Mexican places you guys have in the States."

"Let's go, then!" Tiffany said, clapping her hands. "But first, the jewelry. Oh, Korey, I'm so excited! I really want to find a nice necklace. It'll be the perfect souvenir."

"Have you been to Ensenada before?" Eduardo asked.

"No," Korey and Tiffany said in unison.

Tiffany turned around. "Korey, you told me you *had* been here before," she said.

"Well, I was on a cruise like this one, and the ship only docked here. I didn't get off."

"You didn't?" she said, giving him a funny look. "I thought you had."

"No, I stayed on the ship," he insisted. "I didn't go ashore."

"Here is the agua fresca place," Eduardo announced, pulling up to a small building on a street corner. "The lime-kiwi is the best."

"Okay, let me get them," Tiffany said, jumping out of the car.

Korey stared moodily out the window. Ensenada really hadn't changed. It was just as dirty and rundown as he remembered it.

Tiffany returned with three large cups filled with ice, lime-green liquid, and chunks of fruit.

"I got one for you, Eduardo."

The driver smiled. "*Muchas gracias*, Tiffany. That is very nice of you."

"My pleasure," Tiffany said. "Now let's go check out that jewelry store!"

They drove around to jewelry stores for the next few hours, grabbing lunch at the place Eduardo had suggested. The food was actually pretty good. After a few *cervezas* with lime wedges, Korey felt like his old self again. There really was nothing to fear. Nobody was following him, nothing was unusual, and Eduardo was being the perfect tour guide. Tiffany had a bad habit of overtipping because she had been a waitress for so many years, but in this case, Korey wouldn't mind Eduardo being rewarded for his excellent service.

Tiffany took some of her purchases out of the shopping bags to admire them once more.

"This painted pot is for my mother, and the ceramic parrot is for my sister," she said.

"That is a particularly nice one," Eduardo said. "See how bright the reds and blues are? The artist used better-quality glaze."

"That's what I thought," Tiffany said. She reached into an orange paper bag with purple ribbon handles. "And this emerald pendant is amazing. I can't stop looking at it." She kissed Korey on the cheek. "Thank you, sweetie."

Korey grinned. "You're welcome. Why don't you keep the jewelry in your purse."

"My purse is too full and the jewelry is delicate. I'll just keep it in all the bags and repack everything when we get back to the ship."

Korey was content. This was an easy excursion. All he had to do was go where she wanted and pull out the credit card as often as she wanted.

"Have you two been married long?" Eduardo asked.

"Just about three months," Tiffany said. "We met at the Luxor in Las Vegas. He's a bartender and I'm a cocktail waitress."

"You look kind of young to be getting married," Eduardo said.

Tiffany laughed. "Oh, you're so sweet. We're both thirty-six."

"Really? You look like you're about twenty-two." Eduardo smiled. "And your husband doesn't look a day over thirty-four."

Tiffany laughed again. "We should bring this guy wherever we go. He's a comedian!"

"Speaking of going," Korey said, "shouldn't we get back to the ship in time for dinner?"

Tiffany ignored her husband. "Wasn't there another jewelry place near here you mentioned?"

"Yes, five minutes away," Eduardo said. He turned to Korey. "Why don't we help your lovely wife carry her things back to the car."

"Okay," Korey said, taking some of the shopping bags.

They went out to the car, and Eduardo loaded everything into the trunk. Tiffany was in high spirits as they drove on to the next jewelry store.

The hours flew by (for Tiffany, at least) and they had dinner together at an excellent restaurant Eduardo said was one of his favorites. They were the only tourists in the place; the rest were locals. Tiffany had her numerous shopping bags next to her on a chair. Leaving them in the car was too risky. "Too many thieves," Eduardo had explained. The three of them ate, drank, told stories, and laughed.

As they drove back to the ship, the sun had already set. They stopped near the entry point of the gangway of the ship.

"We'll miss you, Eduardo," Tiffany said. "If you ever get to Vegas, look us up." She handed him a scrap of paper with her contact info scrawled on it, along with a generous tip.

Eduardo hugged her and shook Korey's hand. He lifted all her bags out of the trunk.

"Do you have everything?" he asked.

"Wait, let me check," Tiffany said.

Korey's hands were full with shopping bags.

Eduardo's phone rang. He answered it. After he hung up, he turned to Tiffany. "The restaurant called and said they found an orange bag with an emerald pendant."

"My emerald pendant!" she cried. "That was my favorite! Oh, let's go back and get it. Right now."

"I'll take your husband back with me instead," Eduardo said. "We'll be the knights to the rescue for the beautiful princess."

Tiffany laughed, flattered at the comparison. "I don't mind going," she said.

Eduardo shook his head. "It's not safe for foreign women to be traveling around the town at night. We men will take care of it."

"Is there a crime problem?" Korey asked. The knot in his stomach returned, and his mind raced for ways to get out of having to go with Eduardo. His head was spinning from all the wine at dinner.

"Look, man, it's Mexico," Eduardo said, as if that explained everything.

"Can't you just—" Korey was going to suggest that Eduardo go get the pendant and meet them back at the dock, but the sharp look from Tiffany kept him silent. He didn't dare suggest they leave the pendant behind. It had cost way too much and Tiffany was already emotionally attached to it.

"There are some things a husband just needs to do for his wife," Eduardo said. "It proves he loves her. Rescuing her emerald pendant from the restaurant is one of those things. Think of how she'll reward you later," Eduardo said with a wink.

"That's right, honey," Tiffany said, kissing Korey on the cheek. "But you two hurry up because everyone's supposed to be back on board in an hour."

"No problem," Eduardo said. "I'll have him back in thirty, forty minutes tops."

"Good," Tiffany said. "I need to shower and change. All that shopping made me tired and sweaty. And I'm getting a headache from all the wine, so I'm going to take a little nap and then get up for the midnight buffet. Wake me up around eleven thirty, sweetie. Don't forget." She quickly kissed her husband goodbye. "And don't you two men get to partying. The ship leaves at eleven sharp. They don't wait for anybody."

Korey watched his wife walk up the gangway, and he ached to join her. The ship was a big refuge, a safe haven. He told himself that in less than an hour, he'd be back onboard, laughing over a drink at his own misplaced fears, waiting for the ship to cast off and leave this place forever.

"Ensenada is a cool place, isn't it?" Eduardo said a few minutes later, speeding through the dark streets.

"Yeah," Korey said unconvincingly, staring out the window. With Tiffany, he could tolerate it. Now, the place was just grimy and sinister, as it had been all those years ago, and he couldn't wait to set sail.

At the restaurant, the owner handed them the orange bag without a word. Korey checked to be sure the emerald pendant was still there. It was.

Back in the car, Korey heaved a sigh of relief. Eduardo drove silently. Finally, he handed a Polaroid snapshot to Korey in the back seat.

"Who was the man with you in the picture?" Eduardo asked.

"Huh?" Korey said. He took the photo and looked at it. "Where the hell did you get this?" he demanded. Then he realized he was making a mistake. A big mistake. He should have acted stupid.

"I don't know who these people are," Korey said.

"You don't recognize yourself?"

"That's not me."

On some level, Korey knew it was useless to argue. It was a picture of him, age nineteen, on the very same dock where he had earlier that day taken a picture with Tiffany. Next to him was Pete, grinning like the crazy fool he was, also nineteen. Goddamned Pete. A list of problems as long as your arm, and then the bastard had to go and get himself killed a few years ago in a drowning accident. *Drowning*. As if the very circumstance of his death was a reprisal for what he had done here in Ensenada. Punishment for his sin, in other words. Not that Korey believed in sin, per se. Still, it was a scary coincidence.

Korey stared out the window, his mood as black as the moonless night. Finally he said: "It was all Pete's fault. I didn't want to go along on his crazy adventure here. I told him it was wrong. Don't think I haven't been torn apart by it all these years. And now Pete's dead, you know."

Eduardo said nothing.

"How did you know who I was?" Korey asked after awhile.

"You look the same," Eduardo said.

And it was true. The same wide mouth, the same horizontal features.

"How did you get the photo?" Korey asked.

"You never picked it up when you got back on the ship," Eduardo said. "So I bought it from the photographer."

That was true, too. When he and Pete had disembarked that day, the Mexican photographer was right there, snapping pictures, asking for money in return for the photo.

"Later," Pete had said. "We'll buy it when we get back."

But when they returned to the ship, after sundown, the photographer was gone. And too much had happened to worry about a stupid photo.

Pete had tried to cheer Korey up as they both stood on deck to watch the ship pull away from the dock, leaving Ensenada to get smaller and smaller in the distance.

"Look, it was no big deal," Pete had said. "She was just street trash. You think her life wouldn't have ended soon?

These people are so poor, they don't make it to adulthood. Or if they do, they're lucky."

"But she was so young," Korey said. "And that boy saw a lot, you know."

"That's why I asked you to distract the boy. So he wouldn't be able to identify us."

"But why did you even have to do it?"

Pete shrugged. His eyes were as still as frozen water. "I wanted to see what it was like. Live big. That's my motto. Gotta try everything once."

"But it was so wrong," Korey said. "So wrong."

"It was an accident," Pete said. "I didn't mean for her to end up as fish food, but now her parents don't have to worry about another mouth to feed."

"What if they find us?" Korey said.

"Who? The Mexican police? There's no way they'll find us. The whole country is messed up. Just a big trash dump. That's why it was the perfect place to … experiment."

Korey had vomited twice that night. Even all the alcohol didn't blunt the shock of what had happened. Pete was in high spirits, though, and insisted that they stay at the nightclub on Deck 9 until the early morning hours. When they got back to San Pedro, California, Korey almost had himself convinced that it hadn't been real. Nothing bad had really happened. Pete had made it all up to make himself look like more of a badass than he was. He was a big liar. He exaggerated everything. Everybody knew that.

The sound of Eduardo's voice drew Korey back to the present.

"So now," Eduardo said, "I'll be sure to send your wife her emerald pendant. She is a nice lady, very generous. Why don't you write down her address so I know where to mail it."

It took Korey a few minutes to grasp the implication.

"I want you to take me back to the ship," Korey said, with both amazement and pleading in his voice.

Eduardo remained silent, concentrating on the dark road.

"Where are we going?" Korey finally asked, his voice barely a whisper.

"To Ponte Duarte," Eduardo said.

"Look, Pete didn't mean to just dump her there. But he didn't know what else to do with her body...."

"I know," Eduardo said. "But she was my sister. And I've been waiting a long time for this."

"But it wasn't my fault. I didn't *do* anything."

"You *didn't do anything.* Yes. That's the problem. You could have stopped him."

That was true. Korey could have stopped him, but he didn't. Pete had been his friend, and ... well, what was the use now of justifying it? There was no excuse.

Later, when Korey felt the ropes cutting through his wrists and ankles from the weight of the rocks tied to him, and the shock of the salt water on the fresh bullet wounds, in the far distance he could hear the horn of the cruise ship as it pulled away from the dock.

FREDDIE FERNWOOD

4

ALL THOSE RICH PEOPLE looked me over like I was a horse. They wanted to see whether I'd work hard and be a good addition to their stable.

I must have been okay. A guy in a yellow polo shirt slapped me on the back and said: "Well, George Tanner, you're hired. I think you'll like it here. My name's Brady Dolan."

We shook hands. I was now the maintenance man of Spruce Lake. They gave me my own cabin on the eastern side of the lake. Most of the residents stayed from June through August. A few came in May and lingered until October. My job contract started on Memorial Day and ended on Labor Day.

"I built my own deck a few years back, you know," Brady said. His smile was full of camaraderie.

I've met lots of guys like him. Just because they know the difference between a flat-blade and a Phillips, they think they can do construction. When they get themselves in too deep, they want someone like me to come over *right away* and fix their mess. Well, that's what I was hired to do, so I'd have to get used to it.

"Let me introduce you to some of the regulars," he said, leading me across the room.

"I'm Maggie Kirkbridge," said a short, overweight woman with auburn hair. "Welcome."

"Maggie will be calling you every time her toilet gets the hiccups," said another man in a blue jacket. "Name's Tom O'Shaughnessy, by the way." He shook my hand.

"Oh, Tom, please don't spread rumors about me," Maggie cut in. "Anyway, the problem is my septic tank. You do fix septic tanks, don't you Mr. Tanner?"

"Uh, whatever needs to be fixed, I fix," I said. I don't like parties, and I wanted to leave, but they had already put a glass of wine in my hand, and a napkin with little cheesy things.

"And no doubt Freddie will be calling you soon enough with things that need doing," said Maggie, giving a significant glance to Tom. "Are you married, George?"

"Uh, no," I said.

"Maggie, you're not allowed to ask that," Tom admonished her.

"Why not? The interview's over. He got the job." She turned to me. "Freddie will be glad to know you're handsome and not married."

"Who is Freddie?" I asked. "Does he live here at Spruce Lake too?"

"Yes, *she* does," said Maggie. "You'll like Freddie. Everybody does."

THREE DAYS LATER, I got a call.

"Hello?" I said.

"This is Freddie Fernwood," a woman's voice said.

"Yes? How can I help you?"

"I have a hornet's nest under the eaves of the main house. I hope you're not allergic or anything." Her voice was light and low, and she talked fast, like a brook tripping over stones.

"No, I'm not allergic. I'll take care of it."

"When can you be here? I have a terrible fear of being stung."

"If you don't mind, ma'am, the safest time for me to do that would be after sundown, at dusk, when they're less active."

"That's fine."

"Okay, Mrs. Fernwood—"

"Just call me Freddie. I'll be expecting you after sundown, then."

THE FERNWOOD ESTATE was one of the larger properties. To get to the main house, I drove along the gravel driveway through the woods. When the woods cleared, there was the house, and behind it, Spruce Lake.

The lights shone through the windows and open doors, attracting bugs to the screens. I knocked. A tall woman with long blonde hair opened the door. She wore fitted beige slacks and a white button-down shirt with the sleeves rolled up.

Before I could say anything, she said, "Ah. You must be the maintenance man. I heard you drive up. Tell me your name again."

"George Tanner."

"Hello. I'm Freddie." She stepped outside. "Let me show you the problem, Mr. Tanner."

We went out onto the deck. The moon had risen, making a reflection on the smooth, dark water.

"It's right there," she pointed.

I was careful not to get stung. I sprayed it with bug killer, and then scraped off every bit of papery, muddy nest. I refastened some telephone wires under the eaves that had been drooping.

"Well, that's it," I said.

"May I offer you a drink?" she asked.

"As a matter of fact, I could use something cold. I wouldn't mind washing my hands first, if that's okay with you."

"Of course."

We went inside and she pointed the way to the bathroom. It was done in gray slate and redwood, and it looked elegant and expensive.

I went back outside and waited. She came out with two identical glasses and gave me one. On most of the construction jobs I've had, the lady of the house would give us maintenance guys "worker cups." Usually they were disposable. Sometimes they were old, junky plastic things with the writing wearing off that once held a Slurpee from a 7-Eleven or a soda from a ball game. This way, the lady didn't have to worry if we broke them, or stole them. But Freddie wasn't like that. She was treating me like a guest, giving me the same kind of glass she herself was drinking out of.

"Please sit down," she said.

I took a seat in the other Adirondack chair. I tried not to relax too much, because technically I was still on the job, but that's how Adirondack chairs are. The only comfortable way to sit in them is all the way back. I sat back and breathed in the night air, full of moon, pine, and lake.

She took her seat and crossed her ankles. The moonlight glinted off her blonde hair and her long, smooth shins. I could not see her eyes; they were in the shadows.

She asked me questions. She wanted to know where I was from and how I got the job.

"There isn't much to tell," I said. "I was an Army brat. My father was an NCO. We moved around a lot when I was growing up. I dropped out of high school. I've worked construction all my life. I found out about the job here at Spruce Lake from my friend Ray Haupt. Ray built a few of the houses in this area."

"Yes, I know Ray," she said. "He put new roofs on my guest cabins. He also built Brady Dolan's wine cellar. Brady is the wine critic for the *Times,* you know."

"Oh." I took a sip.

"So, tell me, do you plan to make this your career? Fixing things? Is that what you'll do for the rest of your life?"

"The rest of my life is a very long time."

"Yes. But is this what you want to do?"

I shrugged my shoulders. "I'm pretty good at it. It pays the bills. And, it's not as backbreaking as construction."

She was silent a moment, then said: "The problem is, so many people get stuck in things they never thought they'd do. But they stay out of fear. I don't think it's any way to live your life. It makes you smaller." She gave a short laugh. "Now, there I go getting philosophical. I shouldn't do that, because you didn't ask for my opinion."

I took a sip of my drink and looked out at the lake. Maybe it was time for me to go. I started to get up.

She laughed. "Oh, don't mind me. I say things that aren't polite. You just seemed like the kind who probably has dreams and ambitions. I think I saw a glimmer of it in your eyes."

"And … so what if you did?"

She shrugged. "I find that sort of thing … well, it's a good thing. That's all."

I gripped my glass, not sure what kind of game she was playing. Was she coming on to me? I decided to play it straight.

"I guess everybody has dreams and ambitions—including me," I said. "But I try not to talk about personal stuff on the job."

She didn't say anything, but I could feel her eyes appraising me. There was a hint of a smile on her lips.

"Are you always so circumspect?" she asked.

"Excuse me?" I said.

"I said, are you always so circumspect. It means cautious, guarded. Are you always that way?"

"Don't know. Never thought about it. I just try to keep things professional."

"Well, you certainly are one of the more interesting employees we've had here," she said with a laugh.

I wished I knew what she meant. I put my glass down. "I appreciate the drink, Mrs. Fernwood, and I hope you have a good evening. Call me if those hornets come back."

"Good night, Mr. Tanner," she said.

THE PEOPLE AT SPRUCE LAKE kept me busy, but I didn't mind. They weren't a bad group once you got to know them. Maggie was the one I saw the most. She was paranoid about everything going wrong. She'd always apologize for bothering me, and then she'd start gossiping about the other residents.

She recounted the important guests at Brady's wine parties, folks I had never heard of but who were big names in her circle of friends. She told me about the time a bear was on Tom's roof and they had to call animal control.

Somehow she'd always manage to get around to her favorite subject. "And, Freddie, well, she has that reclusive streak to her. Have you noticed? Sometimes I think she calls over repair people just to have company," she said.

My head was under her kitchen sink, and I almost laughed out loud. If anybody called me over just to have company, it was Maggie.

"Now, Freddie is interesting," Maggie continued. "All the men here at Spruce Lake have had something for her at one time or another, but she doesn't seem to be interested. She likes men who ... aren't her peers. Know what I mean?"

I kept working. She sat on a chair nearby, chattering away. I didn't know what she meant, and at this point, with a fitting that wouldn't come loose, I didn't care. She kept talking.

"She's married, you know, but Geoffrey, her husband, is always away. One does get the feeling she has to look elsewhere...."

"Damn," I grunted, while trying to loosen the fitting.

"What did you say?" Maggie asked, surprised.

I got out from under the sink, wiping my hands. "Uh, nothing," I said. "The fitting won't come off."

I rummaged around in my toolbox for the right wrench, and then went back under the sink.

"Well, George, you probably already know that most of the women here at Spruce Lake have a crush on you. You're one of the favorite topics of conversation when the ladies lunch."

I was glad she couldn't see my face. I concentrated on my work, and stayed under the sink until well after she had moved on to telling me how much Brady had spent building his new wine cellar.

EACH PERSON HAD A ROUTINE. I could tell by the time of day who was calling. Maggie called in the morning. Everybody else waited until lunchtime. Freddie called about twice a week. She had minor repairs—a broken door handle or a bent window screen. She preferred for me to arrive around dusk. While I was working, she'd watch. Afterward, she'd bring out drinks and ask me questions about myself and the places I'd seen. We sat outside, in the dark. She'd light citronella candles to keep away the mosquitoes.

One evening she said: "What has Maggie told you about me?"

I chose my words carefully. "Let's see. She says you're one of the more colorful characters here at Spruce Lake."

"Is that all?"

"She says you're dangerous and I should watch out for you."

Freddie chuckled. "She's right."

And then the subject was dropped, and we moved on to other things.

It was a week of hot and humid weather. We were all eager for the rain, but clouds would form and then disappear without shedding a drop. Late Friday afternoon, it looked as if a thunderstorm would be here soon.

Brady Dolan called.

He was shouting into the phone. There was a party in the background.

"Hey, George, I seem to have a loose wire somewhere. Electricity keeps going on and off. And I have a house full of people right now. Can you take a look?"

I drove to his place, keeping an eye on the sky. I didn't like the color, all yellow and gray.

I found the problem at Brady's house and fixed it in fifteen minutes. I told him he should get his electrical panel upgraded.

"Won't you have a drink?" Brady asked. "It does seem to be getting dark awfully quickly, with this storm coming, so you might as well tuck in and have a good time."

"Yes, please stick around," boomed Tom O'Shaughnessy above the din. He and his wife Jean were obviously a few drinks along.

"No thanks," I said. "I have things to do."

An occasional drop of rain fell on the windows. I could be back at my place ahead of the storm if I left now.

"Hey, did Freddie get back?" Brady asked to no one in particular, looking around anxiously. "She took my skiff out onto the lake an hour ago, and now I'm getting worried. I have a motorboat. I should go look for her." He headed for the door.

"I'll go," I said, cutting in front of him and happy to have an excuse to leave. "I'll be right back."

"Thanks, George," said Brady. "You're a pal. But don't do anything foolish, okay? I don't want to go looking for two bodies. Just make sure she's safe, and bring her here," he called after me.

I jogged down the steep path to the lake, watching for the twisted roots and rocks. I went to the end of the pier. She was about twenty yards out on the lake. Her back was to me, but I could see she knew how to handle that boat. She probably took rowing in college, at one of those preppy schools. Girls like her did things like that and did them well.

She expertly guided the boat alongside the pier and turned to look at me. She was trying to catch her breath. The rain was falling in occasional big drops, pelting our heads and making circles on the water. There was a flash of lightning, and a rumble of thunder.

"Hi. Guess I'm getting back just in time," she said, breathing hard. "It's going to be a big one, isn't it."

I noticed how tanned she had gotten since the beginning of the summer. It made her freckles stand out, and even though she was getting a few lines around her blue eyes, she looked young and athletic, like a co-ed. She was wearing a light blue tank top and white shorts. Droplets of water beaded on her upper arm and tan shoulders, mixing with the perspiration. I helped her lift the boat out of the water and put it in the boathouse.

More thunder and lightning erupted, along with a torrent of rain. We stayed inside the boathouse and looked out the windows, but we couldn't even see the trees just a few feet away. The rain made thick sheets of water on the glass. Thunder shook the boathouse.

"No use trying to get back to the main house," I said. "The path was already slippery on the way down. It's a waterfall by now."

"Then we'll wait." She sat across the room, on a pile of canvas tarps, hugging her knees and burying her chin in her arms. Her blue eyes were large, fixed on me.

"Are you cold?" I asked, turning from the window.

She shivered. "Not really. Just don't like all the thunder, that's all."

"Don't worry," I reassured her. "We're safe here. Better than being out on the water." Outside there was nothing but sheets of gray. "You'd have been in real trouble had you stayed out any longer, you know."

"Did Brady send you to get me?"

"Yes." I paused. "Actually, he would've come himself, but I volunteered."

Her eyes were a mixture of amusement and curiosity. "Volunteered. How gallant."

I didn't know what to say, so I stared out the window, trying to see past the rain, but it was no use.

I could feel her eyes on me.

"No need to keep watch," she said. "Nobody's coming."

I turned, and looked into her blue eyes. One, two, three steps and I was sitting next to her on the tarps. She smelled like lake air, clean and tangy. She kissed me. There was no hesitation, no holding back. It was as if we were both nineteen, free from a past we had not lived, eager for what was ahead of us.

I don't know how much time passed. The storm stopped. I stood up and helped her to her feet. She ran her fingers through her hair. We headed back to Brady's cabin. I held her hand the whole way up the slippery path so she didn't fall. I let go when we got close to Brady's house.

"There you are!" Brady exclaimed as he opened the door. "I was worried both of you had been mercilessly lashed by the tempest. Here's a glass of pinot—just the thing to take the chill off."

Freddie accepted the glass with a grateful smile, and took a gulp. I did the same.

Maggie hovered near Brady's elbow, watching us with narrowed eyes. "Did you two get caught in the storm?" she asked.

Freddie answered. "Yes, but in separate quarters. I took refuge in that little shed between here and your pier, Maggie. Didn't think I'd make it back here, and I was right. When the storm was over, I rowed to Brady's boathouse, and there was George, also hiding from the deluge. He helped me put the boat back, and then we came here." Freddie smiled innocently and took another sip of wine.

"I see," said Maggie.

Freddie excused herself and went across the room to talk to other people. Maggie tried to make small talk with me, but I wasn't interested. I tried not to follow Freddie with my eyes, and the effort made me tired. I slipped out the side door when Maggie went to refill her drink.

At my cabin, I lay on my bed, thinking. We had done nothing, really. Our clothes had stayed on. Sure, I would have liked more. But I wasn't twenty anymore, ready to charge when the light turned green and to hell with the consequences. Her husband could have me fired in a minute. Hell, anyone around here could fire me if I took a wrong step.

I dozed off. The phone woke me up. I looked at my clock. Almost nine. I let the answering machine get it. Low voice, talking fast. It was Freddie. I picked up the phone.

"I'm here," I said.

"Hi," she said. "My lights are dead. I think the storm did it."

"Be right there."

SHE FOLLOWED ME OUT to the fuse box and silently watched me work. The air was cool, moist, and breezy. The tension was strong. But I wasn't going to break the ice. That would be up to her.

"Drink?" she asked when I was finished.

"Okay." I tried not to sound too eager.

Rain clouds were gathering again, so we sat in her living room. A fire burned in the stone hearth, making shadows on the wall. She sat on the sofa, in slacks, her long legs stretched out. I sat in an overstuffed chair nearby.

"I don't know who owes whom the apology," she said, "if there is one forthcoming."

"Look, I'll be the one to apologize, if you want," I said. "I didn't mean—"

She held up her hands and shook her head. "Please. No apologies for *that*. Tell me you don't want to risk offending my husband, or that you're in love with someone else, but don't tell me it was a mistake. Or that it meant nothing. I don't want to hear it."

I was silent. After awhile, I said, "Why didn't you tell Maggie the truth? About us being stranded together in the boathouse? We didn't have to give details."

"And invite more gossip? Why do I need to take that risk?"

"I see. Well, you can count on me to be … what was that word you used? Circumspect."

She laughed, and it was a light, musical laugh. I stood up, and suddenly felt very stupid.

"I should go," I mumbled awkwardly.

"No. No, you shouldn't."

WE WERE CAREFUL. Lovers always are. But they fool themselves. They think their secrets stay secret. I spent every night I could with her, in her big bed with a dozen pillows that smelled of her perfume.

She never talked about her husband. I was starting to believe he didn't exist.

August came. I caught myself thinking how I could make her happy after the summer was over. It took me awhile to realize that I was in the danger zone and I had no plan for getting out.

One night Freddie told me her husband would be there the last week of August.

"He usually comes at that time and stays only a week," she explained. "That means we really won't be able to see each other, unless I come to your place. Just for a few hours. But it'll be risky, and I can't promise that I'll be able to pull it off."

I felt like she was stepping on my chest.

"We'll figure it out," I said, trying to catch my breath and think of ways to keep our momentum going. "Why do you stay with him?" I asked. It was a question I had wondered about for a long time.

She shrugged. "I was young and naive when I married him. The money was the magnet. That, and my parents' approval." She laughed and looked at me. "I am honest about that, aren't I? Better to be hated for what you are, than to be loved for what you are not."

"Does your husband know about us?" I asked.

"I don't think so." She shrugged. "I'm sure he's had his share, too."

I HAD MY USUAL APPOINTMENTS at Maggie's. Now I found myself listening closely to her gossip, trying to discern whether anyone suspected our affair and whether I had a chance—a serious chance—with Freddie. The week that Freddie's husband was in town was a week where I had long hours on my hands. I was restless. I took my time working on projects at Maggie's. I didn't want to go back to my empty cabin and think about Freddie.

Maggie talked more than ever, and lingered with particular relish over the subject of Freddie. I kept my eyes focused on my work. But my ears caught every word.

"Freddie's husband, Geoff, used to come to Spruce Lake for two or three weeks, but now he only stays a week. I'd be surprised if they even sleep in the same bed."

"So they fight, probably."

"No, they don't fight, they just stay out of each other's way, if you know what I mean."

"She must love him," I mumbled as I finished putting up some baseboard. I tried to keep my voice neutral. "He is her husband, after all."

Maggie's eyes narrowed.

"Well, I doubt it. I mean, they're apart the whole summer, and when you see them together, there's really no passion. You can tell she's in it just for the money. Freddie cares an awful lot about money." She paused, and added: "If Freddie ever gets serious again, she'd better pick another rich one. She's accustomed to being pampered, and she'd never survive a drop in her standard of living."

"Well, you don't need money to be happy," I remarked.

"You and I know that," Maggie said conspiratorially. "But some people *think* money equals happiness, so for them, it does."

She paused, and then said offhandedly, "Of course, Freddie has been known to dally with men outside her social circles, if you know what I mean."

"Uh, no, I don't."

"Well, she gets nothing from Geoff, except money, so she has to look elsewhere. Fishing in one's own pond is risky because ours is a small pond and word gets around. So she casts her net wide. She's come up with some handsome ones. Mostly maintenance men or gardeners, because those seem to be the most easily available."

She pretended she wasn't talking to a maintenance man, as she arranged some dried flowers in a vase.

"Freddie picks the types who won't blow her cover," Maggie continued. "I'm only sharing this with you because you're my friend, and I know you'd never let Freddie manipulate you." A pause. "Would you?"

I smiled. "Don't worry. I'll watch my head. Otherwise it might join the others on the wall in her living room." I felt as if I had betrayed Freddie by saying this, but I ignored the guilt. I had to watch my own skin, after all. What if I *were* just another trophy?

"I'm only telling you this because I know you have no interest in her." Maggie said. "It'll be our little secret."

THE DAY FREDDIE'S HUSBAND went back to New York was the day I was on O'Shaughnessy's roof, lifting off the skylight to check the seal and recaulk it. I don't know how it happened. I was supposed to see Freddie that night, so I was distracted and in a hurry. Next thing, I lost my footing, fell backward, and crashed through the skylight opening onto the O'Shaughnesseys' kitchen floor. I almost landed on their dog.

I spent the next few days in the hospital with a broken wrist, stitches, and a concussion. I refused all visitors. I got flowers and notes from the folks at Spruce Lake, including letters from Freddie, full of warmth and concern. I didn't want to talk to anyone on the phone, and I couldn't write.

I had a lot of time to think, lying in that hospital bed. I thought about my nights with Freddie. I missed her. Hell, I ached for her. But what more did we really have? Was it love? Could we build anything outside of Spruce Lake, when she was living back in her mansion with Geoff? And if she left him, how could we make our worlds fit together?

I thought about what Maggie told me, about how Freddie would never give up the good life. Money kept her tied to Geoff. What would keep her tied to me? I was old enough to know that sooner or later, the passion wears off, and then you have to get out of bed and actually live with the person.

After I was out of the hospital, I found a small commercial-construction job in Poughkeepsie. I was the general contractor. I had a lot of subs working for me, so I didn't have to do much of the heavy lifting.

I was living in a rented trailer near the site. Freddie drove to see me.

I asked her if she wanted something to drink, but she shook her head.

"How are you?" she asked, sitting at the small table.

"Up and about," I said. "Almost all healed, but I still have to take painkillers some nights."

She took a deep breath. "George, I miss you."

I looked down at the table. Here I was, living in a shabby little trailer that smelled of fried food and cheap paneling. She looked out of place, with her expensive leather jacket and pearl earrings.

"I miss you too," I said.

Her face lit up. "Really? I was hoping you did. Listen, this is important. Geoff has to move to Hong Kong for two years. He wants me to go too."

"Oh."

"I don't have to go," she said. "I could stay back here. I'm not that far away."

Why was it up to me to decide? At Spruce Lake it was easier. There was a routine. Now this was all new. New and risky.

"Well, Freddie, I don't know what to say. I mean, it's your life. Where will you be the happiest?"

Her face fell. For a moment, she looked as if she would cry. But she pulled herself together.

"Where will I be happiest...?" she echoed. Her voice was dull. "I guess that tells me what I need to know." She stood up and walked to the door. "Have a great life, George. I really did ... *like* ... you."

I watched her walk to her car and drive away.

"You dummy," I said to myself. But I didn't call her.

I THOUGHT ABOUT HER A LOT. More than I had a right to. A few months later, I ran into Roy Haupt. We had a few beers together. He asked about the folks in Spruce Lake.

I gave him an update, but I didn't dwell on the details.

Roy smiled when I casually mentioned Freddie's name.

"Now there's a beauty," he said. "Tough one to land, though." Ray was a fisherman, and for him women of her caliber were the elusive ten-pounders.

He sipped his beer. "Picky as all hell, that Freddie. That's why she didn't socialize much. Some called her a snob, but she was always nice to me. Rumors swirled about her lovers, but I never met a single one of those phantom lovers."

"But there was talk...." I said.

"Talk? From that catty little witch Maggie? You can't trust her. She hated Freddie. Maggie was always stirring up trouble with that tongue of hers."

"So did Freddie have somebody? Like Maggie said?"

He gave me a curious look. "If Freddie had a lover, he'd have to be exceptional. She was that kind of a woman, you know."

"Yeah," I said, peeling the label off my beer bottle. "She was quite a woman, all right."

And you're just a dummy, I said to myself. *You let her get away, as sure as if you had reeled her in, taken the hook out, and thrown her back in the lake.*

HIS COY MISTRESS

London, 1906

CHARLES EDWARD JAMESON lit a cigarette and poured a glass of port. He settled against the pillows and listened to the wind.

"I'm glad 'tisn't me goin' out on a night like tonight," Charlotte said. "'Tis a night for the Divil himself."

"Well, then, you are fortunate to stay put," Jameson said, taking a sip of port and letting it linger on his tongue a moment before he swallowed it.

The window rattled again, and a gust of wind found its way in through a gap in the casement, making the curtains move. Charlotte drew closer to Jameson. He put his arm around her.

Charlotte's chamber was a small, cheaply furnished garret room on the top floor of a music hall off Lambeth Road. On the ground floor, actresses and musicians performed in the dance hall. It was a decent venue, clean and discreet. Jameson liked the fact that he could take the back stairs without going through the public areas.

He took a drag on his cigarette. He didn't fancy going out at this hour. But he couldn't stay the night with Charlotte, although he often wanted to. He stroked her thick hair, which was the color of tarnished copper. She was nineteen and reminded him of Lily Langtry, which was why Jameson had chosen her. But beauty alone wasn't the reason. His wife Edith was beautiful, too—even more beautiful than Charlotte—yet he no longer felt any tenderness for Edith.

"When the wind gets bad like this," Charlotte said, "it makes the window rattle. Do ye hear it?"

"Of course I hear it. But you can't let it bother you."

"Nights like this, I can't stand to be alone. Sometimes I go to Maryann's room."

"Maryann? Is she a friend of yours?"

"Yes. Her room is one floor down."

"And she doesn't mind having you room with her?"

Charlotte shrugged. "She's nice enough about it. I can't be alone on windy nights. 'Tis all so ghostly."

"Really, Charlotte. You must get rid of your superstitions. They make you anxious over something as trivial as air."

Charlotte pulled the bedcovers up to her chin. "Must be me Irish blood. Never could stand to be frightened."

"Then it's a good thing you're not in medical school. I have to look at frightening things all the time."

"Like infected wounds?"

"Much worse. Last week, we watched an amputation. Poor chap was a stonemason who got his foot smashed under a load of bricks. The gangrene was already setting in."

"Was he awake?"

"Oh, no. He got anesthetic. But I did see one surgery where the anesthetic was insufficient, and the screams were unbearable. And then, of course, there are the autopsies. One chap threw himself into the Thames, and it took awhile to find him. Dissecting that corpse was like cutting into a bloated sausage."

Charlotte shook her head. "'Tain't right, takin' apart people like that. Desecration, that's what it is."

"It's not desecration. It's progress. Imagine if we could cure a disease because of all we've learned. King Edward's life was saved because he had that appendectomy four years ago."

"And will ye enjoy cuttin' people up?"

"Enjoy it? I'd hardly use that word. It is a skill I must master if I am to become a doctor."

In fact, Jameson found it nerve-wracking to wield the knife, but he'd never admit that to anybody. He had to do it to get through his training. After that, he would be free to open an office in Harley Street—one of the best locations in London—and specialize in the non-surgical aspects of medicine, such as curing fainting spells with hypnosis, or applying poultices to the joints of rheumatic gentlemen. He had recently begun to read Dr. Freud, and he was intrigued by the Viennese physician's theories. Maybe he could eventually specialize in psychiatric therapy, which happened to be a conveniently bloodless branch of medicine.

"And where do ye perform these cuttings?" Charlotte asked.

"There's an operating theater in St. Thomas Hospital." Jameson crushed out his cigarette in the ashtray.

"How many ladies come to watch?"

"None. The only female in the room is the nurse."

Charlotte traced her finger on the design of the red-and-orange coverlet. "Ye could've done somethin' else besides medicine," she said.

"Yes, my mother reminds me of that fact every so often."

"What does she want you to do?"

Jameson wanted to tell her the truth, but he was afraid to reveal too much about the wealthy, prominent family to which he belonged. He didn't believe Charlotte would ever blackmail him, but one had to be careful these days. The fact was, his mother wanted him to live the life of a leisured gentleman, frittering away the hours on the family estate or in private clubs in Pall Mall. But Jameson had ambition. He did not want to slip into the life of dilettantism—or worse yet, affluent indolence—as so many of his peers had done. His mother—and his wife, for that matter—considered "leisure" perfectly acceptable, if not required, for a man of his social standing. He saw things differently, and that created a lot of tension in his family life.

Jameson skipped the details. Instead, he replied: "I studied to become a solicitor, but the law is a crashing bore. So is politics. My true calling is science. Did I tell you I have a keen interest in botany and entomology? I collected specimens while I was in South Africa a few years back."

There was a spark of interest in her eyes. "In the Boer War, then," she said.

"Yes," he said, surprised and gratified at her reaction. "Did somebody tell you about the war?"

"I read about it meself in the paper. Our soldiers gave those Boers what they deserved."

"I didn't know you could read," Jameson said. He immediately regretted his remark. Too late. Charlotte had caught it. Her eyes narrowed and the spark of interest was extinguished.

"Sorry," he said hastily. "I didn't mean it the way it sounded. I didn't think, I didn't know ..." He let his words trail off before he said another stupid thing.

"There's a lot about me ye don't know, Mr. Charles," she said quietly.

He wanted to rekindle her interest so that he could recount his adventures in the Boer War, but she got out of bed and put on a dark blue robe. She sat at her small vanity table and began brushing her long, coppery hair.

He took another sip of port and watched her reflection in the mirror. He suddenly realized he liked her very much—very much indeed. She was beautiful and sensitive, and she had a naïve vitality that he found refreshing.

"You're right, Charlotte. I don't know enough about you," he said playfully. "Tell me about yourself."

"What do ye want to know?"

"Oh. I don't know. Let's see.... What's your favorite color?"

"Yellow, I suppose."

"And your favorite flower?"

She thought for a moment. "Daisies."

"And your favorite dessert?"

"Apple cake. But I'd eat chocolate every day, if I could afford it."

"I like chocolate, too." Jameson finished his port, and decided it was time to get dressed. He went behind the Chinese screen.

"I'm thinkin' I'll go live with me auntie in Dublin as soon as I hear from her," Charlotte said from her vanity table.

"Why is that? Are you not happy here in London?" he asked from behind the screen.

"I like London well enough."

He wished he could see her face. He peeked over the top of the screen, but her back was toward him and he could not see her reflection in her mirror.

"Is there a problem?" he asked.

She was silent. Jameson waited for her answer and poked his head out from behind the screen. "Charlotte, is there a problem?" he repeated.

After a few moments, she said: "No. I miss the green grass of me home, that's all." She shifted in her seat, and her face in the mirror was inscrutable.

"You would tell me if there was a problem, wouldn't you?" he asked gently, trying to catch her eye in the mirror.

She avoided his gaze. "Of course. But, if there was a problem, and I'm not sayin' there is, I don't know what ye'd do about it."

"Well, it would depend on what kind of a problem we're talking about. What kind of problem *are* we talking about?"

"No problem, sir." She resumed brushing her hair.

He finished dressing, came out from behind the screen, and put his hands on her shoulders.

"Out with it, Charlotte. Don't be coy. Is there a problem?"

"No."

"Are you … in a certain kind of … way?"

"No."

He waited.

"I'm always careful," she added, putting down the brush. "I take precautions. All the time."

"Well, that's a relief." He gathered up her long hair and loosely wrapped it around his hand, enjoying the texture of it. "What happens if you don't hear from your aunt? Have you any other family?"

"Nobody worth mentioning." She dabbed at her throat with a powder puff.

"Charlotte, I just want you to know that I can help you. Don't be afraid to ask." He watched her face in the mirror.

She refused to meet his gaze. "I ain't a charity case, sir. Those women who can't feed their own babes, they're the ones who need charity. Not me. I'm a workin' girl, and I make me own way in the world."

"Well, if you need *help*—not charity—let me know."

"Thank ye, Mr. Charles, but I don't need help, either. I told ye, I want to go back because I miss me home. That's all." She caught his eye in the mirror, and added defiantly: "That's the honest-to-God truth. I swear on me mother's grave."

The bitterness of her tone surprised him. She removed her hair from his hands and let it tumble down the front of her bathrobe.

"I didn't mean to offend you," he said. "I'm just trying to help. And I know you're telling me the truth, Charlotte."

Her face softened a little, and a slight smile played across her lips. "I should be grateful. I make a decent living compared to other workin' girls."

"That's true. You have a warm room, and plenty to eat. That's more than a lot of girls have. Yours is not such a bad life."

"No. Not such a bad life."

"I've heard rumors that there are women of my own class in the same profession as yours. They must think it has got its advantages." He smiled, hoping his words of encouragement would put her in a better mood.

She didn't smile, but her tone was half-playful. "Do people in yer class now encourage their daughters to take it up, along with piano and languages?"

For a moment, he thought she was being insolent. But her eyes were downcast, and her long lashes shone against her pale cheeks.

He laughed and put his hands on her shoulders. "Ah, Charlotte. You would make a nice addition to the dinner parties I'm forced to endure."

"I'd like to see those parties."

"They're boring. The people who go have nothing to say. You're not missing anything. Take my word for it."

Jameson bent down to check his reflection in the mirror. He smoothed his collar and gave the ends of his mustache a twirl. He kissed Charlotte on the cheek, then on the top of her head, lingering a moment to remember her scent.

"Good night, Charlotte. Stay well. I'll see you soon."

He left double the usual amount on the bedside table, hoping that would persuade her to stay in London.

THE NEXT DAY, he found himself thinking of Charlotte. If she moved back to Dublin, he'd miss her, and he'd have to start the tedious search all over again to replace her.

Jameson recalled the night when he'd decided to seek out a woman like Charlotte. It was after a dinner dance he had hosted, some months ago. His wife Edith had been witty and charming that evening. She'd held onto Jameson's arm, laughed at his jokes, flattered him in front of the guests. She'd acted as if she were madly in love with him. Jameson wanted to believe, more than anything in the world, that she had warmed to him after almost five years of marriage. She had never been able to conceal from him an inexplicable coldness and lack of interest. He didn't know why she had warmed up that evening, and he didn't care, so long as she had finally decided to love him.

Later, when he was flush with wine and the joviality of the evening, he took a flower arrangement from the table and knocked on her bedroom door. She had insisted on separate bedrooms since their wedding night.

She opened the door a crack. "Yes, Charles, what is it?" He could hear the usual tone of irritation in her voice, and he suddenly felt unsure of himself.

"I brought these flowers," he said, mustering his courage. "I thought we could spend some time together, just the two of us."

"I don't think so. I'm awfully tired."

"But ... we danced so nicely together...."

"Of course we danced. I was trying to keep that horrid Arthur Whitcomb away. And, I made a good impression on Lord Stansbury. He has a lot of influence and can be a useful ally for you, Charles. I think we'll be invited to his next *soirée*."

At that moment, Jameson wondered: *Has she ever loved me?* He didn't know.

He wandered back to his room. Alone, in his bed, he stared at the ceiling. A cold dread gripped his heart as he thought of the bleak years ahead, without intimacy or love, just as the previous years had been.

When he was courting her, her aloofness had been an exciting challenge. He foolishly believed that the more difficult the pursuit, the more satisfying the conquest. On his wedding day, as he walked up the steps of St. George's, Hanover Square, he made a vow to stay faithful to Edith. He thought he was going to be happy with her—or at least satisfied.

But he couldn't ignore the reality any longer. He would never win her over, despite his best efforts. She was not interested in intimacy. She was only interested in the status that came with being married to him.

And that is why he began his search. An affair with a woman from his own class was out of the question. Too much risk. He wanted somebody he wouldn't have to worry about running into at a dinner party or at the theater. He kept a little notebook, written in code and locked away, and rated each place according to certain criteria: whether it was clean and discreet, whether the women were attractive and the right age. He almost quit the whole endeavor when he stumbled upon one place where the girls had not yet reached puberty. But a few more lonely nights and chilly conversations with Edith convinced him that he had to persist. A week later, he found Charlotte.

Now that the months had passed and he was settled into a nice schedule, he didn't want to lose Charlotte. The day after she announced her decision to go back to Dublin, an idea came to Jameson: He would set her up in a small place in St. John's Wood, where certain men of his society kept their mistresses. She could be his, exclusively. The idea made him happy. He thought of the years ahead, with Charlotte there, waiting for him. It gave him a sense of security and contentment about the future that he had not felt with his own wife.

Jameson made plans to tell Charlotte as soon as possible. He was sure she'd accept the offer. How could she not? She'd be far better off at St. John's Wood than she'd ever be in the music hall off Lambeth Road.

The day was a blur of activity, and he hardly gave the matter a second thought. That evening, at home, as he was dressing for dinner, he calculated the hours until he'd be free to head over to the music hall on Lambeth Road. He was meeting friends at the Charing Cross Hotel first. That would require about three or four hours. Afterward, he'd go to see Charlotte. He'd probably arrive at her place well before midnight.

"Knock, knock," Edith announced, strolling through the open doorway of his room. "I didn't realize you were going out. I just disciplined Margaret for not setting a place for you at the table."

"Hello, Edith. Didn't I tell you I had plans? How foolish of me." Jameson stood in front of the mirror, tying his bow tie. He watched her reflection without looking directly at her, and noticed how lovely she looked in a mauve dress, with her wavy golden hair caught up in a fashionable twist.

The words to the Andrew Marvell poem popped into his head:

> *Thy Beauty shall no more be found;*
> *Nor, in thy marble Vault, shall sound*
> *My echoing Song: then Worms shall try*
> *That long preserv'd Virginity:*
> *And your quaint Honor turn to dust;*
> *And into ashes all my Lust.*

He had memorized it when he was at Winchester College. He wondered what Edith's reaction would be if he recited those lines, whether she'd see the irony in the worms trying the "long preserv'd virginity" of a married woman. Perhaps her virginity had in fact grown back from the only awkward wedding-night encounter he'd had with her—like a forest that reverts to a pristine state after years of being untouched. It had been so long since he'd been in her bed, he had begun to believe that the marriage had never actually been consummated, that their wedding night was but a dream. His bitterness toward Edith was soothed by the certainty that he'd soon have Charlotte all to himself.

Edith was rearranging the sterling-framed photographs on his tea table. "No, Charles, you didn't tell me you were going out. You must've forgotten."

"I apologize. I'm sure I told the new maid. What's her name? Margaret, I think."

"You might as well talk to the wall. That girl doesn't remember a thing you tell her."

"Perhaps writing it down would help."

Edith sneered. "She can't read. All the girls from her social class are illiterate."

"Not all."

"Every one that I've seen is," Edith said impatiently. "And it's terribly inconvenient for me."

"Yes, but think of how inconvenient it must be for them."

Edith rolled her eyes. "Really, Charles. I think all that time at the hospital is causing you to rub elbows with the wrong sorts. You've become positively radical, haven't you? Next thing you know, you'll be like that dreadful Gladstone, trying to rehabilitate prostitutes."

Jameson froze. He felt a sudden panic at the thought that she was baiting him. He forced himself to betray nothing, and started over with tying his tie. He glanced at her in the mirror, to see if she had noticed. She hadn't. She was busy checking for dust on the Qing Chinese vase she had bought at Sotheby's. She didn't suspect his activities with Charlotte. He was sure of it.

Jameson's tie was still askew. He loosened it again, and began to tie it again.

"I didn't hear you come in last night," Edith said.

Maybe he had been wrong. Maybe she suspected. Then again, maybe not. Jameson's face didn't change. "Long night at the hospital. Loads of work to complete. I apologize if I forgot to tell you. I could swear I told Roberts, though." Roberts was the butler.

"They're all unreliable," Edith sighed. "Even Roberts, and he's the sharpest of the bunch. Which isn't saying much."

"I'll remember that for next time."

"I've been thinking," Edith said. "It would be nice if we dined together once in awhile, Charles."

Jameson speculated that she was laying the groundwork for one of her latest schemes. Last year, it was a trip to France so she could have several evening gowns made by the best couturiers in Paris. The year before, it was a furniture-shopping expedition in Venice. This year, it might have something to do with renovating the house or buying a motorcar.

"My dear," Jameson said, turning toward her, "we both seem to have different schedules these days. Tonight, I'm going to have supper with George Frederick and Lord Twyndale." He knew this last name would impress her.

Her voice brightened. "Please give Lord Twyndale my best, and tell him he should call on us one of these afternoons. When you're available, of course."

"Of course."

"And," she added, "it might be nice for you to let him know—not in an obvious way, naturally—that we would accept an invitation to the annual hunt at his Bath manor."

Jameson wondered why his wife's main passion seemed to be pursuing social status and approval from people who didn't really care about her aspirations. He thought now, as he had many times before, that if she'd had children to distract her, things might have been different. He wondered why Edith's maternal—and sexual—instinct seemed permanently dormant. He forced himself not to analyze it. It was too painful to dwell on.

"My interest in Lord Twyndale begins and ends with our shared interest in science," Jameson said. "However, if it makes you happy, then I'll drop a hint or two."

"Thank you, Charles. It is the least you can do."

AFTER SUPPER AT THE Charing Cross Hotel, Jameson walked to the music hall on Lambeth Road.

Mrs. Philips intercepted him at the bottom of the stairs. She was a plump woman with short hair and shrewd eyes.

"Charlotte is not well," she said. "Nothing serious. She just needs to rest for a day or two."

Jameson didn't like the fact that Mrs. Philips knew he was there to see Charlotte, but she was the proprietor, after all. It was her business to know these things.

"Do you want me to check in on her?" Jameson said. "I know something about medicine."

"Thank you, but that's not necessary. She's sleeping. But, if you want to make a contribution toward her recovery, I will see that it gets to her." She held out her hand.

Jameson hesitated. He was taken aback by her importunacy, and he didn't trust that she'd actually give anything to Charlotte.

"I'll give it to her myself when I next see her," he said.

Mrs. Philips kept her hand out, waiting for him to change his mind.

He smiled evasively. "In the meanwhile, I should get going." He tipped his hat. "Good night."

He headed for the exit. But when Mrs. Philips disappeared, he turned back and started for the stairs to Charlotte's room, to see what he could do for her. He heard somebody whistling at him. He looked up and saw a pretty blonde girl on the middle landing of the stairs.

"Yer Charlotte's bloke, ain't ya? I've 'eard about you," she said. "Come 'ere a minute. I'll give ya the fill-in."

Jameson hesitated. He didn't really want to go with her. He wanted to find Charlotte.

"Come on," she urged.

He went up the stairs and followed her to her room. It was done up in a cheap imitation of a Paris boudoir.

She shut the door. "Me name's Maryann," she said. "'Ave a seat."

Jameson sat down on a worn café chair. "You're her friend, aren't you? The one she stays with when the wind rattles the windows."

Maryann chuckled. "That's me, sir."

"Is she okay? Mrs. Philips says she's ill."

"Well," Maryann said, "she ain't done 'erself no 'arm, not on purpose-like. Them what works 'round here, they eats. Ain't nobody 'ere a slack-off. Otherwise, it's out the door. On t' other hand, we all get our days when we ain't right."

"What exactly is wrong with her?" Jameson asked.

"Dunno, sir. She just ain't 'er usual self, and she ain't one to lay on to be sick when there's work. She says she don't feel right in the 'ead." Maryann tapped her own forehead. "Said it feels like someone coshed her right between the eyes."

"Did she fall?"

"Naw. I told 'er it'll pass in a day or two."

"I see."

"Yer 'er best customer, and 'er first. She told me 'erself. She says you visit the most often. She don't mind you."

"Does she have a lot of … customers?" Jameson was afraid of the answer, but his curiosity got the better of him.

"Maybe two or three, but they never came back more 'n twice or so. She ain't been at this business long. See, Charlotte likes the stage downstairs. Spends 'er time 'elpin' the girls get ready to sing an' dance. She can do 'air and make-up better 'n anyone. She's got 'erself a tidy little income, 'cause they each have to tip 'er if they want 'er services. Mrs. Philips don't mind, so long as the rent gets paid."

"Take me to her. I want to see her."

"Charlotte don't want to see nobody. You especially. She made me promise not to take you over. Embarrassed, she is. Looks dreadful."

"I don't care how she looks. I just want to help her. I want to make sure she's all right."

"I know that, sir. But she don't want to see you 'til she's better. You gotta respect 'er wishes."

Jameson realized it was useless to argue.

"She'll be better in a day or two," Maryann added consolingly.

"Well, please give her these when you see her." He handed over a small paper bag. "She said she likes chocolates."

"That's kind of you, sir." Maryann smiled. "You came all this way. You don't have to leave so soon." She hiked her dress up to her thighs and smiled.

"Thank you, Maryann, but I'm afraid I need to go now."

"Us girls don't mind sharin'. You're a gent wot knows 'ow to treat a girl, and I'm a girl wot knows 'ow to treat a gent. I can promise it'll be time well spent."

Jameson smiled and gave her a few coins. "Please be sure to give her this. Tell her it's not charity." He added two more. "And these are for you. For being a trustworthy friend."

"Thank ye, sir. And God bless."

"Tell her I have to go out of town this weekend, but I will come see her as soon as I get back."

"Will do, sir. Goodnight."

AFTER HE GOT BACK TO LONDON, Jameson waited a full two days before he made plans to see Charlotte. He had already solved the problem of how he would convince her to stay in London. He was certain he'd succeed. All he needed to do now was wait long enough to be sure she was well enough to accept his proposal.

On Wednesday afternoon, after tea, he was scheduled to assist in the operating theater in St. Thomas Hospital. When he finished at the hospital, he planned to spend a leisurely evening with Charlotte. He would take her to dinner at a small, discreet place not far from the music hall, and tell her of his plans about St. John's Wood.

Jameson was sweating as he walked into the operating theater. He always felt like this when he had to perform a surgery. The beginning of the operation was the worst. He was always terrified of showing bad technique in the initial incisions. But once the body was cut open, and the insides exposed like a carcass of beef, he relaxed a little more. He just had to get through the first few minutes of the ordeal.

The room was shaped like a horseshoe. Four rows of wooden benches circled the perimeter, separated by rails, each row higher than the one in front. All the seats were occupied by men talking to each other. The operating table was in the center of the room, not far from where Jameson was standing, although Jameson refused to look at it until he was ready. Underneath the operating table was a box of sawdust, to catch the blood. A small wooden table nearby held the surgical tools and a basin of water.

Jameson took off his overcoat and hung it on a peg on the wall. Then he rolled up his sleeves and put on a white apron. He wanted to loosen his tie but he knew that would be unbecoming to a man of his social standing.

There was a body on the table, completely covered with a sheet. Jameson was relieved that it would be an autopsy. His surgical technique wouldn't matter as much.

Professor Gibbs came into the room, and the audience became silent.

"Good afternoon, gentlemen," he said to the men seated on the benches. "Let's get started, shall we? Jameson will assist me today."

The professor gestured to the body.

"This should be an interesting case," he continued. "We just got the cadaver this morning. It appears to be an accidental suicide. She was trying for a miscarriage, but she overdosed."

Dr. Gibbs pulled back the sheet and let it fall to the floor. "Pity. She was a beauty," Gibbs said. There were gasps and murmurs in the audience, and one wag made an indecent comment that drew laughter in the back row.

Jameson's mouth went dry, and his legs were weak. Sweat trickled down his forehead.

Professor Gibb's voice sounded far away. "… and I'm sure Jameson will do a competent job. Jameson? Why don't you fetch the appropriate instrument and make your mark."

Jameson's eyes rested on Charlotte's face. He could not tear his gaze away. He wanted to touch her hair, but his arms wouldn't move.

Professor Gibbs put his hand on Jameson's shoulder. "You don't look well, Jameson. Are you able to carry on?"

Jameson continued to stare at Charlotte.

The Grave's a fine and private place,
But none I think do there embrace.

The professor repeated himself. "I said, are you able to carry on?"

Jameson managed to find his voice, which didn't sound like his own. "I'm fine. I'll continue now."

The professor put a knife in his hand.

The theater was silent. Everybody waited for Jameson to make the cut.

The knife clattered to the floor. Jameson bent to pick it up. He grabbed the sheet instead, which was lying on the floor, and threw it over Charlotte. Then he walked out of the theater without bothering to get his coat.

At home, he let himself in and headed straight for his study. He closed the door, got out the decanter of brandy, poured a glass, and drank it in two gulps. He poured another glass, drained it, and loosened his tie. Then he filled his glass with more brandy. He didn't know how much time had passed. He tried not to think.

Edith came in without knocking. She wore a scarlet gown. Her bare shoulders were as white and smooth as alabaster.

"There you are, Charles. I was worried. We have tickets to the Imperial. I hope you hadn't forgotten...." She stopped. "Charles, you've got an apron on."

Jameson stared at her. "That's a beautiful dress, Edith. Is it new?"

"Why no, Charles, I got it in Paris, remember? I wore it to Colonel FitzRoy's party. What's wrong with you, anyway?"

Jameson shrugged and took another gulp of brandy.

"Charles, you don't look well. What have you been up to? Why are you wearing that apron?"

"There was an autopsy today, Edith. Quite fascinating. She was a prostitute. Pregnant." Jameson felt his throat getting tight, and he fought the urge to cry. He wondered if it would have been a boy or a girl. In his mind's eye, he could see the child playing with Charlotte on the green grass in St. John's Wood. Jameson would have been very happy, even if the child were a bastard. It would have been his.

"Well, take off that apron and let's get going," Edith said. "We're going to be late."

Jameson didn't budge. He lit up a cigarette and blew the smoke out forcefully, watching Edith's face.

In a hoarse voice, he said: "She was trying for a miscarriage, but she took too much of whatever potion she had concocted. The trick is to become sick enough to expel the foetus without actually killing yourself. It's easy to miscalculate."

Edith recoiled. "That's disgusting, Charles. I don't want to hear any more about it. Why don't you get ready so we can go."

"She didn't mean to kill herself."

Edith glared at him. "Well, what can girls like that expect? It's part and parcel of the life they choose to live."

Jameson put down his cigarette, took off his apron, and came over to Edith. He circled behind her, admiring the perfection of her neck, and the way her golden hair fell in little ringlets at the nape.

"And do you know why girls like her are in business, Edith?" he said softly.

Edith stiffened. "Because they like what they do. Otherwise, they wouldn't do it, would they?"

"I'll tell you why. It's because men are despicable creatures. They need an outlet. If their wives don't provide it, they turn … elsewhere."

Edith broke away from him and whirled around. Her face was a mixture of horror and defiance. "I don't need to know any of this!"

"Oh, yes, you do. Women like you are the reason for women like her."

"How dare you compare me to a common slut!" she screamed.

His voice was almost a whisper. "When I was courting you, you pretended that you desired me. As soon as the wedding band was on your finger, you treated me as an accessory in your wardrobe, to be taken out for show when you had a social engagement, and then ignored when the guests were gone. You didn't marry me because you loved me. You married me for the wealth and the status and the endless rounds of invitations."

Edith took off her wedding band and put it in his hand. "Take it, then."

Jameson caught her wrist. He put the ring back on her finger, a little too forcefully. She winced.

"'Let us sport us while we may, like amorous birds of prey,'" he quoted.

"What does that mean?"

"I'm going to be more of a husband. And you're going to be more of a wife."

He grabbed Edith and kissed her. He liked the fact that he no longer cared what she thought about him. He pushed her onto the sofa and found his way through her petticoats.

Afterward, he lit a cigarette and swirled brandy in his glass.

Edith sat on the edge of the sofa, her back toward Jameson. She arranged the folds of her dress back into place and fixed her hair.

"I'll get ready now," Jameson said. "Tell Roberts to bring the carriage in ten minutes. We don't want to be late for the theater, now, do we?"

IN MEMORY

WHEN TERENCE TRONG tried to kill my brother Bertie, I managed to cultivate a certain gratitude toward Trong. During our therapy sessions, it was easier to interact with Trong if I remembered the good that had come out of this tragedy. Were it not for him, Bertie and I would still be estranged.

It all started in 2034, the year our mother died. By that time, Bertie had legally changed his name to Byron Skye, a stage name he'd adopted when he'd begun his career as a guitarist ten years before that. Against long odds, he managed to attract fame and success, along with the drugs, alcohol, and promiscuous groupies that are the not-so-fringe benefits of such a career. Byron Skye was now a musical legend in some circles, and an idol to the alienated teenagers who found salvation in his songs. But to me, he would always be my little brother Bertie.

And he would always be irresponsible. Once our mother's modest estate was settled, he burned through his share of the inheritance in a matter of months. Bertie said it went toward new stage equipment. I figured it had gone up his nose or into his veins. He asked for loans. I said no. We argued, then stopped talking, except through lawyers. Eventually, even that stopped. I often saw his picture in local entertainment weeklies. His image appeared in white ink on black T-shirts. Once or twice I was tempted to see him on stage. But I didn't go. I told myself it was because I didn't enjoy loud music in crowded arenas, but the truth was, too many hurtful things had been said between us, and I just couldn't face him anymore.

Then Trong came into our lives.

Bertie was found comatose in a high-end Boston apartment. It took the surgeons thirty-six hours to replace the damaged part of his spine, C6 through T7. I went to see him as soon as I found out what had happened. I didn't tell the nurses that he was my brother. For the first few weeks, I shared the visiting hours with his groupies and party friends who came to cheer him up. They arrived in cliques, tattooed, pierced, and boisterous. The women clutched stuffed animals and polyester roses in gaudy colors; the men surreptitiously brought bottles in brown paper bags. They gave me funny looks, but mostly ignored me. I tried my best to be the overweight, boring, middle-aged guy who sat in the corner reading.

Eventually they stopped visiting when they realized Byron Skye wasn't going to recover anytime soon—if at all. Five weeks later, Bertie woke up. I was sitting in a chair next to his bed, reading *Memory Isolation: Theory and Techniques* by Jonas Bernard. Neither of us mentioned our past grievances. We were on the same side now.

Terence Trong was not only my brother's attacker. He was the primary suspect in his own wife's murder. Bertie was the one who found the dead woman's body. He still has night-mares about it, even during the day, when he is awake. It is common to suffer extreme shock under those circumstances. The shock was even worse because the murder victim had been Bertie's lover.

TERENCE TRONG SAT IN a chair facing my desk. He helped himself to the dish of candy next to the desk lamp.

I shuffled a few papers. "Tell me, Mr. Trong, what do you remember about March twenty-fourth, 2054? That would have been the Friday you found your wife Marcy in the apartment, dead."

Terence Trong drew his black eyebrows into a frown. "Well, all I remember is being in my office, like I told you before. Then I remember calling a cab for the airport. I don't remember anything more. It's all such a blur. I mean, I was under a lot of stress."

I watched his face carefully. It was a handsome face, smooth and tan. His mother was from an affluent Manila family and his father from Hong Kong, but Trong had been raised in a wealthy suburb of Boston. His life of pampering showed. The chin and cheeks were getting flabby.

"What about the pizza?" I asked.

Terence Trong looked puzzled, not in the least uncom-fortable, as if we were discussing somebody else. "Yeah, they say they found my saliva on one of the crusts in the box. But I don't remember actually eating the pizza. I love pizza, so maybe I just ate it out of habit, because it was there, without really thinking about it."

"A strange reaction, don't you think, Mr. Trong? To eat a slice of pizza while your wife's corpse is just a few feet away?"

Trong let his eyes wander to an invisible point near the ceiling. "I can't explain it. I just don't remember the pizza. I don't remember that day, or the weeks that followed."

No question about it. His memory isolation was first-rate. He must have paid a lot of money to have his brain altered like that.

"Do you still remember Marcy?"

"Oh yes," he said. "Even now, I can't believe she's gone. I loved Marcy, you know. I loved her so much." His face crinkled in anguish, and he choked back the tears.

I looked at the well-manicured hands covering his face. Those were the same hands that had murdered his wife and mangled my brother. And yet, without the memories, was he really the same man?

The truth was, the memories were not actually gone. They were isolated somewhere in his brain. Terence Trong had paid a specialist to sever the neurological connections so that he could not access them. So long as those connections remained severed, the memory, for all practical purposes, was lost.

But it was possible that something could spark a connection. Perhaps some of the severed neurons had even started to regenerate—although there was no evidence that it had ever happened in a case like this. Even so, if I could find the right stimulus, I might be able to access the memory. Or, more accurately, I might be able to get Trong to access it.

And what were my qualifications for testing this theory? I had none. My specialty is midlife depression and divorce stress syndrome. I knew nothing about memory recovery until Trong became my patient. I arranged to get myself assigned as his therapist by pulling some strings in the psychiatric community. Of course, nobody knew about my personal stake in this case. I didn't disclose the fact that Byron Skye was my brother. To Trong's high-powered lawyers, I was an undistinguished forty-something shrink looking for a little career excitement. They figured I was the perfect candidate for the job.

I spent most of my time listening to Trong as he chattered on and on about his father's import-export business and his mother's social connections. Trong liked to pretend that his father's company would have collapsed years ago had it not been for him. The truth was, Trong played at working like he played at everything else: to suit himself. He could wake up one morning and decide he'd rather spend the next year or two lounging on the Riviera. He was rich enough and capricious enough to do it, and he wouldn't have given it a second thought. Our little therapy sessions would have been abandoned long ago, had it not been for one small snag: The court said he had to show up for every session—including additional ones, if I deemed them necessary—or else be institutionalized. The threat of losing whatever freedom he still had was the only thing that inspired him to come to my office on a regular basis.

I often let him talk, hoping for some slip, some clue that his memories were returning. Sometimes I tried to chip away at the memory block directly.

"Can you tell me about Byron Skye?" I said the name as if it meant nothing to me.

Trong took a moment to collect his thoughts. "That would be Marcy's lover, right? I never knew his name until all this happened." His gaze shifted toward the thick file on my desk.

I sighed, pretended to be bored, and checked my watch. "But had you ever seen him before?" I asked.

"I told you. I had seen him in the restaurant with Marcy. They were holding hands. It was so obvious what was going on." Trong's dark eyes narrowed, his jaw clenched, his hands curled into fists.

Time was not dampening his anger. I made a mental note to introduce the subject on a regular basis. It might yield something after all.

"Infidelity is one of the worst forms of betrayal," I remarked. "One really never gets over it."

"You're speaking from experience, then," Trong ventured. I could see he wasn't really interested in what I had to say. He was just tired of doing all the talking.

I sighed. "Yes. My wife left me after we'd been married only three years. That was eighteen years ago. But that doesn't diminish the injustice, or the pain of it, does it?" My eyes rested on the heavy crystal candy dish at the edge of the desk. It had been a wedding present.

Trong was restless. He looked at his watch.

"Time's up," he said. He got to his feet and paused at the door. "Nice to see you again, Dr. Quinn. I'm off to the Keys this weekend. Some friends are racing their boats."

I remembered the days when murder suspects with memory problems were detained in mental hospitals until they were well enough to assist in their defense. Now, things were different. A man like Terence Trong was free to go as he

pleased—even to yacht races in Florida—so long as he came back in time for next week's therapy session. Periodically, a panel of psychiatrists had to determine that Trong posed no danger to himself or to others. His lawyer had made sure the right psychiatrists had been hired to do the evaluation. Trong came through with flying colors every time.

※   ※   ※

I LEFT MY OFFICE AFTER DARK, when the rain had started again. I checked the car's anticollision settings, punched in my destination, and headed out to the Westbury Medical Center.

The glare of headlights reflected off the wet road and made my eyes ache. I reached in my pocket for my pills and took two without water. Then I decided to let the car go on autopilot. I pressed a button on the console and reclined my seat back, watching the drops splatter on the sunroof as the car sped through the darkness.

I mentally reviewed today's session again, going over every detail so that I could detect the hint, the allusion that might give me the smallest entry into his memory. I couldn't find a thing. Six months of intensive therapy, and I was still no closer to that memory than I was the day he first sauntered into the office with his designer sunglasses and polo shirt.

The car's chime signaled that we had arrived at Westbury. The car pulled into the parking lot and stopped near the door, waiting for me to get out so it could roll forward to park itself in the appropriate space.

The rain was now a drizzle. I ran to the lighted glass doors of the building, avoiding the puddles on the sidewalk.

I stopped in the waiting room to shake my umbrella, and then went upstairs. My wet shoes squeaked as I walked.

Heavy table lamps, paintings of English cottages on the butterscotch-colored walls, gold drapes dotted with small blue flowers—all these things made the place look more cheerful than it really was. Byron was sitting in the far corner, making adjustments to the newest guitar he'd built. His hair was tied back into a ponytail at the nape of his neck, but some of it still escaped and hung in front of his eyes. He looked up when I sat nearby.

"Hi Leonard," he said.

"Hi Bert. That's a remarkable design you have there." I gestured to the guitar.

"Yes, isn't it?" Bert said, fingering it. "I altered the acoustics a bit by changing the shape of the sound hole. I also reconfigured the cutaway. And I used black walnut in some of the inlays. For aesthetics. See?"

"May I try it?" I took the instrument and strummed a few notes. "I like the tone. Vivaldi's mandolin concerto would sound interesting on this."

Bert shook his head. "No. It's not meant for classical stuff. Just modern." He peered at my jacket. "You have water on you. Is it raining?"

"Yes. It's been raining all day. See how the window is wet?"

Bert glanced at the window, which was dotted with rain and illuminated by the lights from the parking lot.

"Oh. I guess it is," he said. "I didn't realize it was night already." He turned his attention back to the guitar. He played a few riffs, his fingers dancing nimbly across the strings, and the other people in the room stopped to listen.

I noticed that he was keeping his nails clipped. That was a good sign.

Then he put the instrument down. "I have a few other designs I want to try." He rummaged in his bag for sheets of paper with drawings and notes, and spent several minutes explaining his ideas.

I observed him, watching how the twitches and tremors in his head and hands hadn't improved since last week. The doctors didn't know whether his motor skills would ever be normal again. But Bert was lucky to be alive and walking. The artificial spine seemed to be taking hold quite nicely.

After awhile, I looked at the clock. "Are you ready for dinner, Bert?"

"Dinner? I thought it was lunchtime."

"It's dinnertime now." His sense of time was distorted. He did not remember that he'd just observed that it was dark outside.

"Okay. I'm ready." Bert stood up. He suddenly turned to me, and his face was full of apprehension. "Listen, Len, I don't want to talk about it, okay?"

I smiled and patted his shoulder. "No problem. We won't talk about it, then."

We strolled down the long hallway. There was a time when Bert's body was conditioned and muscular, when he walked with the grace of an athlete. At the height of his career, he could do backflips on stage with a guitar in his hand. Now he was skinny and slightly hunched. His head bobbed, and he shuffled a bit when he walked, like an old man.

I guided him to a corner table in the noisy dining area. Bert seemed happiest and most relaxed with lots of people around, even though he didn't socialize much anymore. We chatted about music, Bert's favorite topic.

An attractive woman in a medical uniform walked by our table.

"That's Marion Marzetti," Bert remarked. "She's a doctor. But she's not my doctor, unfortunately."

"She's not bad looking."

Bert laughed. "I don't date doctors, as a rule. Things get too complicated. But you can ask her out if you want. I think she's single." Then his face got serious. "Marzetti reminds me of Dolcetti's. Dolcetti's was the place where Trong saw us."

It always started like this. Something triggered Bert's memory, and then he'd start talking.

I waited.

"But I don't want to talk about it," he insisted.

"I know, Bert. You don't have to."

"But I don't know if I told you that Trong was doing weird things, like snipping pieces of Marcy's hair while she slept. He made her wear the same perfume, use the same shampoo for months on end. She thought he was into voodoo or something. Now we know he was doing it so the memory alteration would work."

I'd heard this part of the story before, dozens of times at least. "Well," I said, "the trick is to find actual solid evidence that will hold up in court. Weird behavior isn't enough to convict him. Even something as obvious as that."

Bert took a bite of his hamburger and talked while chewing. "Yeah, you said that before. Did I tell you the name of the pizzeria we ordered from that day? Costanza's. The place burned to the ground, which is too bad, because they had the best pizza. I heard they're opening up a new one called Mama C's." He paused. "And I remember what was on it. Just cheese and pepperoni, no hot peppers. Marcy never ate hot peppers, which is strange because she was Thai, and Thai people usually like spicy food."

I smiled and decided to try to steer the topic to happier memories. "Do you remember when we were growing up and you used to always pick the peppers off your pizza, even though you always insisted on ordering it that way? Used to drive Mom crazy."

"Yeah," said Bert. "I liked the residue of taste, but I hated to actually eat them."

"You were a weird kid," I teased.

"But without me to harass you, you wouldn't be where you are now, would you?" Bert joked.

"No, I would not." That's how the two of us now talked about our shared history. We made little jokes, we alluded to our past, we danced lightly over the dramatic moments, but we never really discussed the worst times between us. I often wondered whether Bert recalled those bad times, or whether his perspective had changed and it no longer seemed important.

I smiled at my little brother. "You know, Bertie, I spent a lot of time talking to Mom about you. She never got over the fact that you changed your name."

Bert grinned. "I know. She used to harass me about it." He imitated his mother's voice: "'Bertrand Quinn, I'll never understand why you got rid of the perfectly good name your father and I gave you. Byron Skye sounds like the name of a gigolo.'" He paused for effect. "So I said: 'But an expensive gigolo, right, Mom?' She didn't think that was so funny."

I chuckled. "You always knew how to say the right things, eh, Bertie? Mom would get off the phone with you, and for the next hour, I had to listen to her rant and try to calm her down."

"That's why you're a good shrink now. If you could do therapy on Mom, you could do it on anybody."

"That's right." Then I started to think aloud while I shook salt on my baked potato. "I just wish Trong would blab as much as Mom did. Then I'd have something to go on."

It took me a few moments before I looked up and saw that Bert had buried his face in his hands. His shoulders shuddered as he sobbed.

"Come on, Bertie, everything's okay," I said, reaching over the table to put my hand on his arm. "I'm sorry I mentioned him. It was thoughtless of me."

"I miss Marcy. I wanted to marry her."

"I know you loved her, Bertie."

"He had to take her away from me. Why did he have to do that, Len? I couldn't even recognize her. Her face was destroyed, her long hair soaked with blood.... I understand why he wanted to kill me. But he didn't have to make her suffer."

I squeezed his arm, as if I could press understanding into him. "Terence Trong doesn't think about other people. He only thinks about himself."

"Yeah, you've explained that before," Bert said. "But how do you hurt and kill the thing you love? I could never hurt her."

"When Trong uses the word 'love,' it's not the way we mean it. For him, 'love' is more like obsession and control.

He's a different creature, Bert, and you'll never understand him. You leave that kind of understanding to me, okay?"

Bert clenched his hands in frustration. "The thing plays over and over. Like, I'm in the middle of putting a guitar together, and I let myself think about it. I see her so clearly, in that damned apartment. Twenty minutes have passed like that"—he snapped his fingers—"and I thought it was only a few seconds." He ran his hands through his hair, causing more of it to come loose and hang in his face.

I leaned closer and said in a low voice, "Why not have the memory erased? It would save you from so much suffering."

Bert sat silent a few moments. "It would betray her," he said finally.

"All memory of her wouldn't be erased—just the traumatic one. The happy memories could stay. Then she'd always be with you, in a good way."

"I'd be denying the reality of her death."

I shook my head. "No, you wouldn't. Nothing will change the facts. You'll know what happened, but you won't keep reliving it."

Bert rubbed his face. "I don't know. What if a key thing— the thing that could hang Trong—what if that gets erased, too?"

"I don't think it will," I said. "We've been through it all dozens of times. You told me everything you remember, everything that could get us somewhere. You never even saw him come up behind you."

"That's right. I let myself in, and found her on the living-room floor. Next thing I know, I'm in a hospital with a new spine."

I took a cup of coffee and a slice of lemon pie from the automatic dessert cart that came drifting past the table.

"So, how about if we have the worst parts of the memory erased," I said. "You'd sleep a hell of a lot better."

Bert shook his head. "It's cheating. Like Trong cheated. I'd be no better than he is."

"There's a world of difference between you and Trong. He erased the memory to escape the consequences of his actions. You'd be using it to escape the pain and suffering he caused you."

Bert pushed his plate aside. "But, Len, don't you see? We *are* our memories. That's all we have to define who we are." He gestured around the room. "All these people here are collections of memories. Their memories are what give each of them their uniqueness. I know I sound crazy, but I've thought about this a lot."

"I can see that. I've thought a lot about it, too," I said, taking a forkful of pie. "But you don't have to keep a memory just because it's yours. You can get rid of it, like you'd get rid of a bad tooth. Technology can help you. Why not use it to make your life better?"

Bert slumped back in his chair and stared despondently at the table. "I don't know. There is this sense of ... karma. I keep thinking I need to remember everything—as punishment, maybe?—for something I've done in this life or in a past life. Maybe it's because I was an adulterer. She *was* married, you know."

I took a sip of coffee. "Look, Bertie, forget about the 'past life' nonsense. Reincarnation doesn't hold up under scrutiny."

Bertie frowned. "What do you mean?" he asked defensively. "It makes a hell of a lot of sense to me."

"You know, it's interesting," I said. "In ancient Greek mythology, when people died, they went to Hades. There, in the underworld of the dead, were two rivers. If you drank from the river Mnemosyne, you would remember everything you ever knew—including your past lives. If you drank from the other river, Lethe, you'd forget everything. The dead souls who were destined for reincarnation gathered at the banks of the river Lethe. They were waiting to return to this life. But before they were allowed to do so, they were required to drink from the Lethe."

"Why?"

"So that they would forget their past lives before they returned to this world. They were wiping the slate clean, so to speak." I paused. "You mentioned karma. Eastern religions also stipulate that in order to be born again, you must forget your past lives."

"So what's that got to do with Trong?" he asked.

"Suppose we could reincarnate Trong into a miserable life and a violent death. That would be great, wouldn't it? Well, according to the rules of reincarnation, he'll have no memory of his transgressions in *this* life. He won't be able to make the connection that his suffering is linked to what he did to Marcy. He won't even know who Marcy is. Where's the justice in his punishment if he can't remember *why* he's being punished?"

"There's cosmic justice," said Bert. "He'd still be paying for what he did."

"But if he doesn't even *know* it, how is that fair? Justice requires that you know what you did wrong—and I mean to really know it, by remembering. Otherwise, punishment is not punishment; it's sheer cruelty. If you had a dog that chewed your furniture, and you waited a month to punish him for it, that would be cruel—and not very productive—because the dog can't remember what it did."

Bert shook his head. "Look, if I knew Trong was going to be reborn into a hellhole, I'd be happy. He deserves it."

"Okay, then Marcy was evil in a past life and she deserved her violent end in this life."

Bert's eyes flashed with anger. "That's a lie! Marcy was the sweetest, kindest person on the planet. There's no way she could ever be evil, in this life or any other."

"How do you know? The rules of reincarnation say you can't know that for sure, at least not in *this* life. That's why reincarnation makes no sense to me."

"Then why do people believe it?" Bert challenged.

I shrugged. "Probably because it seems to offer an explanation for evil and injustice. People believe a lot of stuff that doesn't hold up under scrutiny."

Bert didn't look convinced. "In the old days, Trong would've been locked up until he could remember something."

"You're right. But the Supreme Court decided that the old way is wrong. Their logic is basically what I was just arguing. If a person can't remember *why* he's being punished, incarceration—even if it means being confined to a mental hospital—is cruel and unusual punishment, according to them."

Bert traced an invisible design on the tabletop. "But Trong could be prosecuted if there's proof that he intentionally had his memory altered, right?"

"Absolutely." I sipped the coffee. "But there's no solid proof—yet. There's just a flight record of his chartered plane, a limousine rental in Freiburg, and a load of excuses about grief and healing. Until we have more to go on, Trong is free to live the good life, chatting with me in therapy during the week, and then jet setting with his rich friends every weekend. Probably not what the justices had in mind when they penned their decision. But that's the loophole, and Trong and his lawyer were smart enough to take advantage of it."

"Why can't the court just order him to undergo memory reversal?"

I chuckled dryly. "Ah, yes. Lead him to the waters of Mnemosyne, and force him to drink. If only I could do that. But I can't drop an electrode into his brain and go fishing for lost memories. It's against the law."

"I don't understand why they can't just put him on trial. The evidence is there."

"The district attorney doesn't think the court would accept the circumstantial evidence—not until his memory is restored," I explained. "That's why no case has been filed. Personally, I think the DA is a bit too cautious, but I'm not a lawyer. I will say this, though. The DA was smart enough to put Trong under the jurisdiction of the court and make him do therapy with me. Trong has no choice about that. Trouble is, he's a tough nut to crack."

Bert rubbed his chin, thinking. "How long before you give up?"

"Give up? Oh, I'll never give up," I said. "So long as the memory remains isolated, he'll never see a jail cell, much less stand trial. But he will have to stay in therapy with me as long as I'm alive. And he knows it. So his job is to keep from remembering. My job is to force him to remember."

"How did you get him as your patient?"

"I have friends in high places. I pulled the right strings." I didn't feel like explaining the details.

Bert's faced darkened. "You didn't mention the fact that we're related? The nurses in the hospital didn't seem to know."

I put my finger to my lips. "Shhh. Nobody asked."

Bert lowered his voice. "And if anybody finds out it's my brother shrinking Trong's head, what then?"

"Then things will get … interesting. But let's not worry about that right now." I patted my jacket pocket, searching for my pipe. I settled for a pack of mints I found at the bottom of one of the pockets. "No, dear Bertie, I'll never give up on Trong. Never."

THE SESSIONS WITH TRONG were the same, week after week. My approach was dry and professional. I was the tired old shrink going through the motions of the assignment. I often allowed Trong to leave a few minutes early. I didn't reprimand him when he was late. I never scheduled extra sessions. That helped Trong to relax a bit more. He figured I was too weary and indifferent to be a real threat. He liked to recount his latest adventures with his rich friends and beautiful lovers around the world, careful to stress that his romantic conquests grew only out of a need to fill the painful void in his life. I tried to steer the conversation to more promising areas, such as Trong's jealousy over Marcy and Byron, but that didn't yield much. It usually annoyed Trong and made him impatient.

"Why do you always want to bring up Marcy and that pig?" Trong demanded one day. "I want to get over it, okay? The past is the past."

"As a psychiatrist, I think it's an important area to explore."

"My lawyer might differ with you there. Be careful, or you'll be charged with coercion."

"And then you'll have to start all over with another therapist who might insist on more sessions per week and the full ninety minutes. How tedious would that be?" I gestured to the minicam on the side table. "Your lawyer can look at the tapes of our session anytime. I've got nothing to hide."

"Yeah," said Trong. I could hear the retreat in his voice. "He's busy. I'm busy. But he'd be here within the hour if he thought something was wrong."

"I'm sure he would."

The Trong family fortune undoubtedly kept the lawyer at Trong's beck and call twenty-four hours a day. I looked at my watch. "We still have about thirty-five minutes. I need to eat something. Do you mind if I eat lunch while we chat?"

"Not at all," Trong smiled.

I added as an afterthought: "Care to join me? My secretary always orders more than I can finish."

"I guess so." I'm sure Trong figured he'd be expected to do less talking if he was busy eating.

A few minutes later, Stephanie brought in two small tables with napkins and silverware. As she was serving the pizza, Trong asked her, "Where'd you order this from?"

Stephanie glanced at me.

I answered. "I believe it was from a place called Mama C's. Isn't that right, Stephanie?"

"Yes," said Stephanie on cue, "I go there all the time. I think it's the best."

"I'm sure you know what you're talking about," said Trong. "You'll have to take me there sometime, Stephanie. I love to try new places. Especially with new friends." He smiled his most charming smile.

Stephanie smiled cordially and closed the door as she left. I knew she was not impressed with him. She always rolled her eyes behind his back when he came in for his appointments.

We ate in silence. I pretended to review my notes, but I was watching a small monitor built into the surface of my desk that showed what the minicam saw. So far, nothing about Trong's demeanor was different.

"This is good pizza," said Trong. "You know, my lawyer said I should never eat or drink with you because you might slip truth serum into my food."

"Good thing he's a lawyer," I said, "because he doesn't know a damn thing about medicine. Truth serum is crude technology, and it has a high failure rate."

Trong laughed. "Yeah, well, he believes in conspiracies. He's always worried about people plotting behind his back. I told him to run a company and try getting people to do their job, and then see how much chance there is that the idiots will cooperate enough with each other to hatch a conspiracy."

"Speaking of conspiracy," I said, "tell me who you think killed Marcy. You saw her dead on the floor. Did anyone spring to mind?" I hoped the combination of pizza and suggestion would jog something in his memory.

Trong finished chewing and wiped his mouth with the napkin. "I don't know who did it. I think it might be that Byron Skye. He would've had a motive."

"But he got attacked too."

Trong shrugged. "I haven't worked it out. Look, I know the evidence seems to point to me, but I didn't do it. I have no clue who did." He certainly looked convincing. There was not the slightest sign of guile in his face or tone of voice. Taste and smell, two of the most evocative senses, were having no effect on Trong's recollection.

I tried a different angle. "Tell me again why you went to the Freiburg Institute of Neurological Sciences to get your memory altered."

He was unfazed. "Well, as I told you before, I had been there before and after she died. I have nothing to hide. I went there before because there was this old flame from my past who was getting in the way of my relationship with Marcy. I thought if I had her erased, it would make my marriage better. But the guy at the institute said there was no way he was going to tamper with that. Too risky, given that he'd have to wipe out so much memory. I mean, I knew the woman for over two years, and that's a lot of stored information. Then, after Marcy died, I was in so much pain, I went to Freiburg again to see what they could do for me. They said they couldn't touch me so long as the investigation was ongoing."

"So why didn't you come back to the States right away? You were gone over a month."

Trong shook his head. "Couldn't bear it. Just being anywhere on the East Coast made me miss her. Our stomping grounds were from Bar Harbor down to Miami. Marcy loved the coast. As for our apartment here in Boston, forget it. I could never set foot in there again. I left the furniture and all the dishes. Too many memories."

"What kind of memories?"

"Everything that happened before she died."

"Tell me about it."

Trong looked at his watch and tossed his napkin on the table. "I wish I could, but time's up. Thanks for the chow. See you next week."

I spent the rest of the evening finishing the pizza and going over the video for any sign that Trong's memory was coming back. I looked at the face, gestures, posture; listened to voice inflection, his choice of words. I could detect nothing.

I TRIED TO SLEEP on the airplane. I put the magazine over my face and inserted noise-canceling earplugs. The man next to me kept asking the flight attendant for another drink, and clumsily made his way to the bathroom every half hour, it seemed, bumping me in the process. I needed to get to the hotel as soon as possible for a hot bath, an hour in a massage chair, and a real bed. I was getting too old for the discomforts of travel.

The hotel outside of Freiburg sat high on a hilltop in the Black Forest. It looked like a modern museum pretending to be an Alpine lodge. Two-story walls of shatterproof glass faced the German countryside, and the steep steel-reinforced gables of the glass roof sliced into an overcast sky. The ridges still held a mantle of snow from the last storm.

Inside, the hotel was posh. From the comfort of the arm-chair in the lounge, I liked looking down on the Black Forest. The deep blue shadows were beautiful and not at all menacing from my vantage. I had no desire to go hiking there, though. I'd never enjoy myself: I'd be too worried about getting back to the hotel before sunset. I thought about being lost there, having to spend the night in the dark forest, shivering in the frigid night air. My heart constricted. I took a sip of my drink and nestled more firmly into the chair, grateful for the blazing fire and the staff of attentive waiters nearby.

Early the next morning a car came to take me to the Freiburg Institute of Neurological Sciences. The day was sunny and a little warmer, and I kept the window rolled down a crack so that I could enjoy the smell of the forest.

Ever since Trong had become my patient, I had hoped that my skill and experience as a therapist would make him remember. I'd read everything I could lay my hands on about the mechanisms of memory isolation and recovery. I called colleagues for their advice, and adapted my thera-peutic techniques accordingly. There simply wasn't much data out there. Oh, there was a lot of speculation, theory, and predictions, and some case studies, but no really good longitudinal studies of what happened when people got their memories isolated. There weren't many experts, either. The technology was relatively new and growing all the time. I decided to see for myself what the director of the Freiburg Institute of Neurological Sciences had to say. That's why I was in Freiburg. A visit might give me new ideas for deal-ing with Trong. After all, Trong had been there. What did I have to lose?

The institute was an industrial-looking building built into the side of a forested hill. The interior had the stark, white-and-gray sterility of a scientific building.

A trim woman in a dark blue suit greeted me from behind an information desk.

"You must be Dr. Quinn," she said with a light accent and a cold tone. "Welcome. I'm Monica. I'll take you to Dr. Bernard." I found her stiffness off-putting, and I could see a flicker of disdain in her eyes as she appraised my obviously out-of-shape physique.

She walked down a nearby corridor, and I followed. We stopped in front of the elevators. "We can take the stairs if you like," she suggested.

"I hate exercise." I smiled and pressed the call button. "I prefer to let the elevator do the work."

She ignored my comment.

As we waited, a man in a custodial uniform opened up a panel in the wall nearby and began working on the machinery inside.

As we stepped into the elevator, I remarked to Monica: "Having building troubles?"

"We have state-of-the art technology. But from time to time, it does require maintenance."

"I thought it was a bit chilly in here."

"He's repairing the air-filtration system," she added, clearly reluctant to give me even this much information.

"Oh."

It was something I hadn't noticed until now: the building had no smell whatsoever—no carpet odor, no disinfectant scent from cleaning products, no residual odors from building

materials. I was about to ask more questions, but Monica was talking again as we approached Jonas Bernard's office.

"Dr. Bernard will be happy to show you more," she said. "I hope you enjoy your visit." She turned and walked away.

DR. BERNARD WAS A tall man with heavy brows, a toothy smile, and a crushing handshake.

"Nice to meet you, Dr. Quinn. What kind of a doctor are you?" He had a faint European accent.

"Psychiatrist."

"Are your patients children?"

"No. Why do you ask?"

"Because I have a special sympathy for children. It's so sad when they must come here, although they do amazingly well in our program. Are you here on behalf of one of your patients?"

"Not exactly," I said. "It's my brother, actually. He had a traumatic experience, and I want to see if anything can be done."

Bernard tilted his head and regarded me for a moment, as if trying to decide whether I was telling the truth. He probably had visitors who claimed they were there on behalf of somebody else when they were actually seeking treatment for themselves. No matter. Let him draw whatever conclusions he wanted.

"When did this traumatic event occur?" Bernard asked.

"About a year ago."

"Let me show you around, and we can talk more about it."

Bernard held open the door as we walked in and out of various rooms. Some were filled with medical equipment and computers. Others were elegantly appointed hotel suites with beds and entertainment equipment for music, movies, and computer games. One large, sterile room was a state-of-the-art surgical center with the latest technology, including gamma knives, several brain scanners, and monitors. We surveyed the room from the glassed-in viewing theater.

"This is the heart of our operation," said Bernard, gesturing at the room on the other side of the glass. "This is where we work our miracles."

"You mean, where you erase memories?"

"Well, erase is a misleading word. Essentially, we find the memory, and then we cut off all connections leading to it. The memory becomes isolated. It's still there, but it can't be accessed. So, from a functional standpoint, it is erased."

"How do you locate the memory?" I asked, fascinated by the monitors and computer equipment.

"I'll show you." Bernard took me to an adjacent room. He taped some electrodes to my head, and put a scanner near my skull. "Now, let's have you think of something poignant. How about ... the most embarrassing thing that ever happened to you."

I closed my eyes. How far was that? Too many years to count.

"Tell me what you're thinking," said Bernard.

I hesitated. Even now it was painful to recount. "I was ... I can't remember how old. I think I was nineteen or twenty. I really liked this girl—Jessica. One night she and her parents took me out to dinner. Nice restaurant, very fancy. I drank too much. I got sick and vomited all over the table. With her parents sitting right there. God. It mortifies me to even think of it." I opened my eyes and took a deep breath. Bernard was watching the screen.

"Yes, I can see the region on your brain where that memory is stored." Bernard pointed to the image. It was a model of my brain. One spot glowed more brightly than the others.

Bernard continued. "I can also see the pathway as you accessed that memory. Here, we can go back and replay it." He pressed a few buttons, and the brain on the screen glowed with shifting colors that corresponded to brain activity as a recording of my voice was telling the story.

"If you wanted to have that memory erased," Bernard explained, "you'd be in our surgical room, conscious, and we'd go through it in every detail. And the gamma knife would sever those pathways that get you to the memory. You wouldn't be able to access it anymore."

"And the gamma knife is accurate?"

Bernard smiled. "It goes only where I direct it, almost on a molecular level. No incision. We don't even shave off your hair."

"How do you make sure you've severed all the connections? There's more than one way to a memory, you know."

Bernard smiled at the observation. "Of course. Just as there are many routes from here to Berlin. That's why proper memory isolation takes several sessions over several weeks. We activate every pathway that might lead to the memory, and cut it off. It would be like finding every highway, every street, every alleyway, every forest footpath that could lead from here to Berlin, and blockading it."

Bernard gestured to the screen again. "In your case, I might have you remember the dress and jewelry she was wearing that night. If you brought a scarf of hers with the perfume still on it, all the better. We call those 'props.' Any props you had that could bring back the memory—a copy of the restaurant menu, a picture of her, perhaps, the wine you drank—we would encourage you to bring so we could use it in the memory sessions."

"How about the shampoo she used, the clothes she wore, a snippet of her hair?" I was thinking about Trong's behavior in the months before he killed Marcy.

"Anything that evokes the memory. We encourage patients to bring things that have a scent. For some people, scents are the most evocative. We're often not aware that there is a smell associated with a particular memory until it happens, and suddenly, we're transported back to a place we hadn't thought about in decades: our grandmother's kitchen, for example, or a childhood amusement park."

I peeled the electrodes off my head. "I noticed there are no odors in this building. Is that because smell is so evocative?"

Bernard nodded. "Exactly. When our patients undergo memory isolation, the process itself can interfere with the result. If, for example, I was in the middle of erasing your memory and the smell of damp earth came in through an open window, it is possible that you would be able to access the otherwise isolated memory when you smelled damp earth. We have no proof that this has ever happened, of course, but we can't be too careful. In fact, no food or drink of any kind is allowed in this building. No plants or animals, either. The windows don't open and the air is constantly filtered. The cafeteria is in a separate facility. Anyone entering a room where we are having an active session must scrub down and be deodorized."

"How do you know where to direct the gamma knife?" I asked, pointing to the screen image of my brain.

Bernard put his hand on another monitor. "This. It's the most advanced functional MRI ever made. It can show images almost down to the molecular level, but we really only need to go subcellular. We see exactly what synapses are activated during the memory session, and we guide the gamma knife accordingly."

"Don't you risk losing other information?"

"Yes. We can't predict what will be lost. But for specific, episodic memories, it is usually not too serious. In your case, you might forget information that's part of the same memory, such as what your girlfriend's parents looked like, what their names were. You might also forget some insight or conclusion you reached that night if it is linked to the isolated memory."

"How many sessions does it take?"

Bernard shrugged. "It depends. We monitor all our patients, including their dream cycles, to see if the memory is somehow being accessed. The average person can be free of one particular memory in a matter of weeks. But if it's a cluster of memories, say, of repeated childhood traumas, memory erasure could take the better part of a year. That, of course, also increases the risk of losing other memories that are stored at the same site or that share the same pathways."

"What about the long-term effects? Suppose the nerves regenerate themselves," I asked.

"Nerves often regenerate themselves," he said. "But they don't reorganize themselves in a way to make access of the memory possible. So, despite the regeneration, the memory stays isolated."

I wondered what kind of data he had to back up his claim.

"But what if they happened to regenerate in such a way that the memory did become accessible?" I pressed him.

"Then we would go back and sever the connections again. But I have never seen such a thing happen. I estimate it would be a one-in-a-billion probability." Bernard paused. "Let's go to my office, shall we? We can chat privately."

We made our way to a large room with a picture window overlooking the Black Forest.

Bernard sat behind a desk. I took the chair in front of the desk.

"Now tell me about your brother," Bernard prompted me. "What kind of memory are we talking about?"

"He found his girlfriend—murdered."

"I see. Is he being charged?"

"No. Does that make a difference?"

Bernard seemed to consider his words carefully. "We don't like to take on cases if the patient is going to be implicated in the crime. On the other hand, it's not our responsibility to do the police's work."

"Suppose you go ahead and do it anyway, and later, you find out your patient is guilty?"

Bernard shrugged. "What can I say? Guilt is a matter of semantics. Most countries won't try somebody who can't remember. By definition, successful memory isolation precludes guilt. We leave the ethical debates to the philosophers."

Bernard was ignoring the moral implications of his own technology. My little brother was wasting away in a medical center with an artificial spine, tortured by his memories. The woman he loved had been brutally murdered, pieces of her face scattered around her own living room. And here was this doctor glibly explaining why the issue of guilt was a matter of semantics.

I controlled my anger and kept my voice neutral. "Let me put it another way. Suppose a person committed a crime and asked you to erase the memory. Would you do it?"

Bernard smiled. "We try to stay out of messy cases like that."

"Because you'd be in legal trouble?"

"Well, the truth is, no outside country, including the United States, has the power to stop us if we decided to take such a case. But we try to avoid situations like that."

I knew there were unspoken exceptions. A building like this was expensive. All that state-of-the-art equipment cost money. Trong's checkbook could easily make it worth Bernard's time.

"Messy cases imply that adequate compensation is in order," I tested.

Bernard smiled again. "That's true whether we're talking memory or gall-bladder surgery, Doctor. Complicated cases run up a bigger bill. I'm sure you see it in your own practice."

"Yes," I agreed quickly. "Yes, although we have so much regulation now."

"Well, we don't," said Bernard, "which gives us the freedom to try cutting-edge things. Shall we talk about how much it would cost for your brother to come here?"

I smiled thinly. "Yes, why not?"

SOMETIME LATER, I went down the elevator. The same maintenance man was leaning into the opening in the wall, cursing and occasionally coming out to mop his sweaty forehead with a damp rag. He kicked the wall a few times, and then cursed again.

"Is everything all right?" I asked in my rusty German.

"The damned air purifier is having trouble again," he said in accented English. "I'm trying to fix it before it burns out again."

He came out and pointed to a large square box inside the opening. "Inside here is a microbial fuel cell. Energy is generated by a special kind of bacteria in a sugar solution. The organism wrenches the electrons from sugar. It's old technology, actually, and not all that efficient, but you know how it is." He shrugged. "The government wanted something environmentally friendly without the word 'nuclear' in it. Anyway, one of the circuits shorted out and started a slow burn. It smelled up the building for weeks. The government inspector came, and we almost got cited for indoor pollution. Dr. Bernard complained. He said the smell was bad for his concentration, bad for his patients. But he's not an allergist, so I don't understand why he cares." The man eyed me suspiciously. "Is he your friend?"

"Not at all," I said. "I just met him today."

The man grunted. "I wouldn't mind being able to walk out of here like you do, and never see Bernard again. But I have kids and a wife. This job pays the bills."

"Well, good luck with the repairs," I said affably.

The man nodded and got back to his work.

After dinner, I sat in the hotel lobby, gazing out of the glass wall that faced the Black Forest. A half moon shined silver on the tops of the trees. Tomorrow, I would fly back to Boston. I went to bed early, but I could not sleep. I kept replaying my conversation with Bernard. I was frustrated because I had learned nothing that would help me make progress with Trong. I slept restlessly, and dreamed of my visit to the institute. I woke every hour or two to check the time, hoping the daylight would come quickly so I could go home.

I sat upright in bed and looked at the clock—5:06.

What had Bernard said? If a certain smell were introduced during the memory isolation procedure itself, it might become a way to access the memory. There was no proof that the mechanism would in fact work that way, but what if…?

I took a car to the institute and waited in the parking lot. The maintenance man arrived at six fifteen. I intercepted him before he could unlock the doors of the building.

"I have something to tell you about Dr. Bernard." I said. I calculated that the man's curiosity about his nemesis would get the better of him.

"Why do you tell me this?" he demanded.

"Because I have my own score to settle. And I don't want you to lose your job."

The man was still guarded. "Why should you care about my job? And why didn't you tell me yesterday?"

"And risk having someone overhear us?"

The man scoffed. "They all know he's no friend of mine. That's why I spoke so freely to you."

"Well, you have your way and I have mine. Let me buy you a cup of coffee."

"I prefer a cup of chocolate in the morning."

"A cup of hot chocolate, then."

The man deliberated. "Wait here. I have to open the building. Then we'll go across the way."

I waited in the freezing air. He returned in a few minutes, and we went to the cafeteria. We sat across from each other with our hot drinks. By the look on his face, I could see mistrust fighting with curiosity.

"Tell me what you have to tell me," he said.

I sipped my coffee. "Why don't you tell me your name first. I'm Leonard."

"Albert."

We shook hands.

"Okay, Albert, let me get to the point," I said. "Dr. Bernard let it slip that he doesn't like the fact that you weren't 'minding your own backyard,' as he put it. It sounds to me as if he has it in for you."

Albert grunted. "So? What else is new? Everybody knows I don't like him, and he doesn't like me."

"What do your other co-workers think? Monica, for instance?" I was fishing for information, for direction.

Albert snickered. "I don't know about Monica. With me, she's professional. I don't think she likes me very much. In fact, I don't think she likes men in general. But as long as she doesn't make my life hard, I don't care."

"Yes. There's nothing you can do about that. You do need to watch your enemies, though. That's my advice."

"You came here to tell me that? Why do you care about my business?"

"Because I want to know why it is that Bernard is so angry at you. Why should he care if the air purifier works or not?"

"How am I supposed to know? Like I said, he's not an allergist. Besides, the smell wasn't unpleasant."

"Tell me what happened."

Albert took a sip of his hot chocolate. "There was a smell in the building. Around Easter. That's when Bernard came down and threatened to kill me."

"Easter," I said, "was that in March?"

"Yes. Easter was on the twenty-sixth of March."

Right around the time Trong was here in Freiburg.

"And what was the smell?" I asked.

Albert laughed. "Madam Malou's."

"I mean, what was the smell in the building that Bernard was so angry about?"

"I'm telling you: Madam Malou's. That's how it smelled."

"Can you please explain that for me?" I was getting impatient, and I was worried about missing my flight.

Albert was clearly enjoying himself at my expense. "Yes. All right, I'll tell you. When I was a boy, I spent some time in Belgium. And in Antwerp, there was this little *confiserie* run by a madam with a large nose and dirty hair. A real witch. But, she made the best caramel. And I mean the best."

"What's that got to do with the building?"

"I'm getting to that," said Albert, drinking some of his hot chocolate. "Anyway, candy making is an art. People tried to duplicate Madam Malou's, but they just ended up with a burned mess."

"So the building smelled like caramel?"

The man rolled his eyes. "This is what I am trying to tell you. Not just any caramel, but Madam Malou's dark caramel with Bretagne sea salt. It came in purple foil."

"How fascinating," I remarked. "Are you sure it was the very smell?"

"I'll prove it," said Albert.

We went back to the main building. Albert opened up the wall by the elevators.

He stuck his hand inside the opening and tapped the metal housing of the generator panel. "If this stupid air purifier could make candy instead of clean air, I'd go in business for myself and give Madame Malou a run for her money. In fact, it still has some of that odor clinging to it."

"Really?"

"Here, take a whiff yourself." He stepped aside.

I stuck my head in the opening. It was dark, and lights on a board glowed dimly. I inhaled deeply. It smelled dusty and electronic, but nothing more.

"Are you sure? I can't detect anything." I pulled my head out.

"Am I sure?" The man repeated, looking as if I had questioned whether he knew his own name. "But of course I'm sure." He tapped the side of his nose with his finger. "I have a very keen sense of smell."

I pretended to be impressed. "Really? But tell me—this candy smell—was it in the building a day or two after Easter?"

Albert grunted. "It was here Good Friday, and for ten days after that. On Easter Sunday, before church, I was here, tinkering with the system. This place was quiet as a graveyard. I didn't think anybody was here. I lit up a cigarette while I was working. It's against the rules, I know, but the air-circulation pump was offline, and what the hell. Smoking calms my nerves. Next thing I know, Bernard is down here, threatening to shove the cigarette down my throat. I guess the smoke made its way through the ducts. He said he'd have me fired. He actually tried to strangle me! He grabbed my throat! But I told him to go to hell. The bastard. My union representative would make his life miserable, and he knows it."

The man reached into the opening and slapped the generator panel again. "It is nothing but a pain, this machine, but what can you do? The government says we must have one, so we have one."

I patted my pockets. "I forgot my pipe. You have one of those cigarettes? I could use one right now."

Albert grinned and fished a crumpled pack out of his pocket. "With pleasure."

I LOOKED AT MY WATCH. Trong was late again. I double-checked that everything was in order. Then I heard Trong's noisy entrance as he started chatting with Stephanie in the reception area.

"Hi there," said Trong, taking his usual seat. His smile was brighter. "Did you read the paper? Christie's is going to auction some Warhol paintings. I've decided to bid, in person. That means I'll have to go to London."

He waited for my reaction. I said nothing.

He continued. "Now, I know I can't skip a single session with you. So, I'll pay for you to go, too."

I sighed and rubbed my forehead. I was still jetlagged. The thought of going to London with Trong was more than unappealing. It was preposterous.

Trong took my silence for deliberation. He continued: "I'll pay everything. I'll put you up in whatever hotel you want. You can eat at whatever restaurants you want—the finest ones in London. They all know me there. We'll meet at our usual time, but other than that, we won't see each other. It'll be a great vacation for you." And he spent the next several minutes elaborating on his scheme, highlighting the attractions of London.

I watched him silently with my fingers steepled.

Trong was a fascinating creature. He was a good talker with an uncanny ability to know what your objections were before you even knew them and to make it all sound so easy, so appealing. It was a masterful sales pitch.

"… and if you need companionship, I know some gorgeous ladies," Trong said. "Of course, if women aren't your preference, we can easily accommodate that," he added, raising one eyebrow.

"I'd like to think about it. In the meanwhile, why don't we get down to business here."

Trong was now in high spirits. He was certain I would go for it. "Sure, no problem. If you have any questions, any special concerns, just let me know. I can arrange it."

I paged through my notes. "Tell me what's been happening in your life."

Trong spent a long time recounting his latest adventures, and he ended up talking about the trip to London.

I listened, then started to probe more carefully, changing the subject. "Have you had any unusual dreams lately—any thoughts or scenes that you didn't know where they came from, just popping into your head?"

Trong took a few moments to think. He shook his head slowly. "No. Nothing that I can think of. Nothing unusual." It wasn't the first time I had asked this question, and he answered it the same way every time.

"Do you still think about Marcy?"

"Of course I think about her. I miss her." His face became long and sad, and he rubbed his eyes.

"Tell me about her."

"It's what I've said before. I loved her. I would never hurt her. I don't care what the evidence is; I'd never kill her. Never. And when I find out who did it, I'll kill him. Personally, I think it was that Skye jerk she was dating."

"Oh? Why do you think that?"

"Because I think he's the type."

"But you said you had never even met him."

Trong's face was smug. "I've been doing some research on my own. I turned up some bad stuff. Drugs, and things like that. Drugs can make a person crazy. That's what I think happened. He flipped out."

I rubbed my forehead. Then I reached for the candy dish, filled with cubes wrapped in purple foil. "Care for one?" I offered the dish to Trong.

"No, thanks."

I paged through my notes. Trong was shifting in his seat, looking at his watch. His mind was clearly on other things, like the upcoming Christie's auction. He was ready to duck out at the earliest opportunity.

I reached for some files next to the coffee machine, and flipped the switch. The machine gurgled and hissed, but Trong didn't notice.

"Tell me about the institute in Freiburg," I prompted.

Trong looked puzzled. "You mean the place that helped me get over my ex-girlfriend?"

"Yes, but I'm more interested in what happened after Marcy died."

Trong took a deep breath. "I told you: they helped me deal with the shock of it all."

Inside the coffee machine, hot water trickled over the candy. I could hear the drip as the watery caramel brew collected in the glass pot. Then I smelled it: dark caramel with sea salt.

"And that would be...?" I prompted.

"The shock—of Marcy's death."

"When did you decide you needed to go there?"

"To Freiburg?"

"Yes. To Freiburg."

Trong thought about the question. "I don't know, exactly. It was all such a blur. The shock was so great. I didn't know what else to do. I was desperate. What is that smell?" Trong's attention was drawn to the coffee machine.

"It's new," I said. "A type of caramel drink. I hear it's quite popular in Antwerp. I'll let you try some in a few minutes, when it's ready. Anyway, why don't you finish telling me about your visit to the Institute of Neurological Sciences. Did you see Dr. Bernard?"

"You know about him?" Trong was surprised.

"Everybody knows who Dr. Bernard is. He's making quite a name for himself these days. Did you see him?"

"Of course. He runs the place, you know. Would you mind turning off that coffee machine? The smell is giving me a headache."

"Not at all," I smiled. I unplugged it and opened the coffee basket. Steam rose. The odor of Malou's caramel filled the room.

"Now," I continued. "Tell me about how he helped you overcome the shock of Marcy's death."

"I don't remember, exactly," said Trong. "It was a very upsetting time. I'd rather not go over it."

I opened a drawer and took a cigarette out of a crumpled pack. "Do you want one?"

"No, thanks," said Trong. He fidgeted. He was casting about for something to do. He reached toward my desk. "I'll try a candy." He unwrapped the purple foil and popped it into his mouth. Then he spit it out. "This stuff is disgusting. Where'd you get it?"

"Madam Malou's in Antwerp. The stuff is really expensive."

"You wasted your money. It tastes like burned sugar."

"Some people like it."

"Some people have rotten taste."

The cigarette smoke drifted around the room. Terence Trong sat on the edge of his seat, ready to leave.

I blew the smoke out toward the ceiling. "How did Dr. Bernard help you to remember what you saw? Did you look at a dress she wore? Did you have a clipping of her hair?"

"A dress? Her hair? Uh, you mean my ex-girlfriend's?"

"Think back to being in the institute. In that big, white room, lying down on the table with the computer equipment all around you, electrodes taped to your head, and hearing Dr. Bernard's voice. Did you bring a sample of Marcy's perfume? The shampoo she used? Did any of that help you to remember?

Scent evokes memory, you know. Or maybe the building had a peculiar smell that day...." I inhaled and blew out more smoke.

Trong ran his hand through his hair and swallowed a few times. His dark eyes were large. He looked at his watch. "I don't know what you're talking about. Time's almost up."

"We still have fifteen minutes. Think, Terence. Think about what it was like in the institute as you relived what you saw when Marcy died."

"I don't want to. It's too painful." He scowled defiantly.

"Just tell me what you remember. Tell me what you saw."

"Okay, I'll tell you. I saw blood. Smashed face. Hair spread out on the floor. Blue dress. Blood on it. I told you all this before."

"What did you do next?"

"I don't remember. I had to get out. I couldn't stand seeing her like that. It was too much. Oh, God, I don't know why it had to happen like that." Trong covered his face.

"Byron Skye comes in. What did you do next?"

"I don't remember." He lowered his hands and clenched them into fists.

"Skye didn't even see you, did he?"

Terence Trong looked up. There was a look of rage and desperation in his eyes. "He did it, you know. He's the one who killed her. He came back to see his handiwork. I didn't want to tell you any of this until the detective got more evidence, but there it is."

"You must've been startled to see him at the apartment."

"Yeah, and that's why I grabbed the paperweight. I was afraid for my own life. It was self-defense."

"You were afraid he was going to attack you."

"If he could do that to Marcy, he could do it to me. So I hit him with it."

"You wanted to make sure he wasn't moving."

"Yeah, I was afraid he'd get up and come after me. I got scared, okay? I panicked. I gave a few more blows than I should have. I may have even used my foot once or twice."

Terence Trong didn't realize he had just confessed to a crime.

"How did he get into the apartment?" I asked.

Trong's eyes narrowed in fury. "He had a key. *She* gave it to him. They thought I was stupid, but I knew. I knew *everything* about the two of them. I had pictures. You had to see how bad she cheated on me. Was there anything she wasn't willing to do for him? *To* him? The whore. She thought that beautiful face of hers could make anybody do her bidding, but I showed her. And when *he* saw her all smashed up, with that beautiful face ruined, well, that made it all worth it. *That* was the moment." Trong grinned triumphantly. It was chilling to see.

I pretended to be unimpressed. "Was it worth it, for that moment?"

Trong shook himself, as if waking from a trance. "It was a blur. A total blur. I don't even know how she got there. Don't know how Skye got there. The intruder must've been hiding out in the bedroom. I think it could have been the pizza-delivery guy. They ordered a pizza, you know. I got out of there as fast as I could. I was really scared. I though he'd come after me next."

Trong blinked rapidly. Perspiration shined on his forehead. I could see he was trying to do the calculations, trying to find out where to go next.

"Did you use the paperweight on Marcy first?" I asked.

"It already had blood on it. Slippery. I had to wipe it off to get a good grip when Skye came after me."

"Now that's interesting. You were acting in self defense, but you took the time to wipe off the weapon because it already had blood on it."

Trong smiled, and I could see he was thinking of an escape route. "You're right. I misspoke. It was a blur, you know. I just can't remember. I'll have to tell the detective to investigate the pizza-delivery guy. The damned cops don't do their job, do they? You have to do it for them."

"I agree, Terence. That's why you're my patient. I got tired of waiting for the cops to nab you. Had to do it myself."

"What the hell are you talking about?"

I smiled. "Didn't I mention that Byron Skye is my brother? Nobody in the world has a greater interest in getting you to remember than I do. And now that you do remember enough to hang yourself, my job is finished."

I was enjoying the reaction in Trong's face. The rich brat was not getting his way. The murderer was starting to see the gallows.

"Not that I wish you anything but the best," I said sarcastically. "With your money, they'll probably send you to a nice jail, maybe one with swimming privileges in the afternoon, and a cellmate who doesn't stink too much. No more winters on the Mediterranean, though. Life's going to get tough for poor Terence Trong. And who knows how pissed off the jury will be when they find out what you did. They don't like rich jerks like you who think you can treat people like dirt and then buy your way out of trouble with memory alterations. They might just decide that a lethal injection is what you need to put you out of your misery."

The last thing I remember was the fury on Trong's face as he came across my desk.

I woke up in the hospital with a splitting headache.

Bertie was in the chair next to my bed, softly strumming his guitar.

"It's about time you woke up," he said. "You've been out for two days."

I felt my head. A bandage covered most of it. "How bad is it?" I asked.

"The doctors say you'll survive. And our friend Trong is in custody now. He says he's going to sue you for unprofessional conduct and lying about the fact that you're my brother." Bertie looked worried.

I waved my hand, which was threaded with intravenous lines. "Let him do what he wants. As long as he goes to jail, I'm happy."

"But what if they don't let you practice anymore? What if they take away your license?"

"I wanted to retire anyway," I said. I looked around. "How did I get here, by the way? The last thing I saw was Trong in a rage."

Bert's face was grave. "He broke a candy dish over your skull. Your secretary came in when she heard the noise. She saw him pummeling you, and ran out to call the police. They found Trong a few blocks away, wearing your blood." Bert paused. "I hate to tell you this, but he did a number on your head."

"I did a number on his, too," I chuckled. "I got him to remember just enough to hang himself."

Bert threw his head back and laughed with total abandon, the way he used to when we were kids. It was the first time I had heard him laugh like that in a long time.

My own laughter threatened to become tears. I swallowed the lump in my throat and changed the subject. "I could use some dinner. Care to join me for a bite?"

"It's only lunchtime," said Bertie. "But I'll call and have them bring two sandwiches. Then, after lunch, I'll show you my new drawings for a bass guitar. I think it's going to be my best design yet."

7 REPENTANCE

WHEN I GOT A JOB as a nurse's aid at the Rosa Caplan Nursing Home, my grandmother asked why I wanted to work at a place that didn't even celebrate Christmas. I told her a job was a job, and it was a nice place.

"But you know how di Jews are," my grandmother said. She still had her Polish accent, even though she'd been living in the United States since she was a teenager. "Dey don't like Catholics."

"They treat me fine, Baba."

"Dey tink dey the chosen ones."

"They're *old*," I said to my grandmother, as if that would settle it.

"I old too, but I don't tink myself special."

"Anyway, I don't care about stuff like that, Baba," I explained. "This is 1988 already. We're modern now."

"You wear your gold cross, di one I give you for your First Communion," she told me. "And don't let dem tell you anytink about Jesus."

I wore the crucifix the next day. Nobody cared, not even my nursing supervisor Adele Stein. She herself wore a Star of David all the time. After that, I realized I had nothing to prove, so it didn't matter if I wore it or not. I usually left it at home, in my jewelry box.

I came to like and respect most of the residents. There was Mr. Rozenberg in room 212, a former concert pianist who actually listened to modern music. We had a lot of conversations about Linda Ronstadt and Whitney Houston. Then there was Mr. Ganz, in room 201, from Poland. He was very quiet, no trouble at all, and he once asked me whether I had ever tasted *makowiec*—poppy-seed cake. I told him my baba makes it all the time, and I'd bring him some. Mrs. Fischer in room 122 liked to talk about her days working in the Sylvania electronics factory in the 1940s. Miss Pearl, in room 117, was always crocheting socks for her nieces and nephews.

But the most interesting—and repulsive—resident was Dottie Luger, a fat Polish woman in her late sixties. Even when she wasn't talking, she was the center of attention for one reason or another. She could dress herself, but she often wanted one of the aids to help her. Dottie's personal hygiene could be a problem—especially in hot weather—if nobody made her wash. Her hair was often greasy, and it never got combed unless one of the nurses or aids combed it for her. She pretended to be more helpless than she was, except when it came to taking care of Mrs. Shapira.

Dottie always hovered near the reticent Mrs. Shapira. Mrs. Shapira's white hair stood up in tufts on her head, like a cockatoo's crest. She pulled at it from time to time, not saying anything, just sitting there blinking her blue-lidded eyes. Occasionally she wiped her long, beaklike nose with a handkerchief. You could tell that Lucy Shapira had been beautiful in her youth. Now, she was a quiet, wispy feather, drifting down the corridors in her wheelchair while Dottie Luger pushed her along, talking enough for the both of them. When the weather was good, Dottie wheeled Mrs. Shapira outside to the front lawn so she could sun herself. She made sure Mrs. Shapira didn't get too much sun, and she fetched her a glass of water when she was thirsty.

Once, Mrs. Shapira's middle-aged daughter came to town to visit her.

"Who are you?" Mrs. Shapira said to her daughter in a whispery voice.

"I'm Mimi, your daughter."

"Oh, no," said Mrs. Shapira, smiling gently. "You are pretty, but my daughter was very, very beautiful. You cannot be her."

Mimi came out of the room with tears in her eyes. Dottie Luger, who had been lurking just outside the room and heard everything, tried to comfort the stricken daughter.

"Don't worry," Dottie said with her heavy Polish accent. "She don't know me most days, and I her best friend here."

Dottie liked to talk to Mrs. Shapira because Mrs. Shapira was probably the best listener Dottie could find. Everybody else had lost patience with her. Mr. Ganz resolutely ignored her. The only time I ever heard him talk to her was when he told her to shut up and go away when she tried to engage him in conversation. Mr. Rozenberg once remarked that you knew when wind was breaking in the room because Dottie's mouth was running. Even the normally chatty Miss Pearl fell silent when Dottie came around, her crochet hook working furiously as she tried to ignore the woman.

I chalked it up to the usual squabbles among cranky old people living together. I didn't mind Dottie. At least she was alive and robust, and nothing I did as a novice nurse's aid threatened her hold on life. Some of the other patients, like the comatose Mrs. Levine in room 110, were completely unaware of their surroundings. Mrs. Levine had been bedridden for a long time. Each time I gave her a bed bath, rolling her skeletal body first to this side and then to that side, I worried that I would sever the invisible strand of spider's silk, the one that kept her barely tethered to this world, and that I would send her soul soaring into the next world. I did not want to be the one to break that tether.

Adele Stein noticed how gingerly I treated her.

"Darlene, she's not bone china," Adele Stein said to me.

"But she's so weak. I'm worried I'll hurt her," I said.

"Just be sure you're moving her properly, and don't let her stay in any one position too long. We need to keep those bedsores to a minimum."

Adele Stein never assigned tasks to another nurse or an aid that she wasn't willing to do herself. She gave sponge baths, administered enemas, started IVs, spoon fed the residents who couldn't feed themselves, and changed bedsheets and diapers.

Adele Stein had high standards of professionalism. She didn't gossip, and she didn't tolerate unflattering nicknames for the residents. A frustrated nurse's aid once referred to a deaf, incontinent resident as "old poopy pants" and we all got a lecture from Adele on why it was important to respect the dignity of every person at the Rosa Caplan Nursing Home.

In Mrs. Levine's room, Adele bent over the unconscious woman. "Mrs. Levine, I don't know if you can hear me, but I'm going to move your arms and legs to get your circulation going, okay?"

Mrs. Levine didn't respond, of course. I tried to be as vigorous and confident as Adele was in moving those weak, flaccid muscles, but I was still worried I'd damage poor old Mrs. Levine.

Trina Johnson, another nurse, hurried into the room and announced breathlessly: "Dottie took Mrs. Shapira for a walk again to Nazareth. We just got a call from one of the nuns."

Nazareth Nursing Home was a Catholic facility a half a block away. It was one of Dottie's favorite destinations.

Adele rolled her eyes. "Not again." She turned to me. "Darlene, would you mind collecting her?"

"Okay," I said, relieved that I didn't have to keep exercising Mrs. Levine.

I walked over to the nursing home. A nun greeted me at the front door. She wore a calf-length black habit and a black wimple that covered her hair. A large silver crucifix hung around her neck.

"I'm Sister Bernadette," she said cheerfully. "I haven't seen you before. You must be new."

"I'm Darlene. I just started a few weeks ago."

"Well, Dottie was in our chapel again," Sister Bernadette explained. "She visits us from time to time. She was telling her friend, the one in the wheelchair, all about Jesus and Mary and the Act of Contrition. I always find it remarkable that a Jewish woman like her would know all that."

"Dottie is from Poland," I said. "Some of the Jewish residents told me they learned about Christianity in the countries where they lived. Mr. Blum—he's one of our residents—he lived in Italy for fifteen years. He speaks fluent Italian and knows all about the Vatican." I pointed to myself. "My last name is Ruminski. The only Polish I know is the swear words … which I don't say," I added hastily, in case the nun was offended.

Sister Bernadette laughed. "I say swear words all the time, especially when I bump into things, but don't tell the mother superior."

A nurse came down the hallway with Dottie, who was pushing Mrs. Shapira's wheelchair.

"Hello, ladies," I said. "I'm here to take you home now."

"Oh, did you bring di car?" Dottie asked.

"No. We're going to walk," I said. "It's not far."

"Oh. Okay." She leaned over to Mrs. Shapira. "We go home now, Lucy."

Mrs. Shapira sat blinking and wiping her nose.

"Goodbye, ladies, and take care." Sister Bernadette waved to us as we left.

As we walked down North Street, Dottie was in a particularly chatty mood.

"You di new girl," she observed.

"Yes, I just started a few weeks ago."

"You know about my family?" Dottie asked.

"I don't think so," I said, navigating Mrs. Shapira's wheelchair over a bump in the sidewalk.

"Nice husband I have. Smart. Handsome. My little girl, angel. Three years old. Curly red hair, like a doll. Rosy cheeks. Plump little arms. And my son, seven years old. Handsome and smart like his father."

She was obviously caught in a memory warp by the way she described the ages of her children. That was common among many old people.

"They must be all grown up now," I said, trying to bring her back into the present. "Do they live here in Buffalo?"

"Oh, no," she said. "All dead. Di German soldiers come. Dey shoot my little girl at the front door of house. Her little head falls on doorstep, di curly hair in a pool of blut."

Dottie bent to pick up a dandelion. She twirled it between her fingers and continued her account. "My husband and son upstairs. Dey no come down. Di soldiers set fire to house. Di smoke gets my husband right away. My son, at window, screaming, tears on his little cheeks, as flames come near. Di soldiers have their guns ready, pointed up at him. Dey tell him if he jump, dey shoot him like pigeon. I watch his hair catch fire. I watch him burn, screaming and crying."

I turned to look at her walking beside me. How could she be so casual, describing this horrible tragedy?

She was looking at me, watching my reaction. Her smile was tight, her eyes glistened, and she blinked rapidly. I concentrated on maneuvering Mrs. Shapira's wheelchair over the bumps in the sidewalk. Then we were at the edge of the lawn of the Rosa Caplan Nursing Home. The day, which had been sunny and pleasant a few minutes ago, was now clouded by Dottie's tragic story. The blue sky was darker. The twittering birds were far away. I heard notes of despair in their song.

"Dottie, I didn't know any of this," I said. "I'm so sorry. Where did this happen?"

"Lodz. Nineteen forty-one. Dey killed Jews, you know. But everybody doesn't want me to talk about it. So I don't talk about it."

"You were lucky to escape. I'm sorry about your family." That's all I could think to say.

"Yes. I escape," she said. She leaned over to Mrs. Shapira and said: "We home now, Lucy."

AT NINETEEN HUNDRED HOURS, Adele Stein got ready to go home. I still had two hours left on my shift. In the corridor, I almost bumped into Trina Johnson, who was coming out of Mrs. Levine's room.

"She's on her way," Trina Johnson whispered solemnly. That meant Mrs. Levine was dying.

"And we've got a fun night ahead of us," Trina continued. "Two aids called in sick. Bedpans need to be emptied. Somebody puked in the hallway, housekeeping is supposedly on the way, and I still have to pass out meds and get some of the night owls settled down for bed."

Adele Stein walked over to us and said: "I'm going to punch out, then I'll wait with Mrs. Levine. She shouldn't be alone. Darlene, please help Trina get things squared away."

Sometime later, Trina and I had managed to restore some order.

I went into Mrs. Levine's room. Adele was still there. The old woman was barely breathing. Adele was holding her hand.

"It's a matter of time—a few hours at the most," Adele said quietly.

"The daughter will be here soon," I told her, "and the son is flying in tonight." I paused. "Do you want me to sit with her while you take a break?"

"Thanks, but Mrs. Levine and I got along great, back when she was … with it. She would want me to stay."

I thought of Dottie and her tragic past, and how her story had cast a shadow on my day, although I had been so busy this last hour that I'd hardly had time to dwell on it. I was silent for a while, listening to the late-evening quiet settle into the nursing home. Two doors down, Mrs. Samson was talking on the phone, while Mr. Rozenberg shuffled by with his cane, whistling a song.

"I was wondering," I said. "Why do we call Dottie by her first name, but all the other residents are called 'mister' or 'missus'?"

Adele Stein shrugged. "We've always called her Dottie. A good name for that senile old bat, don't you think?"

Her answer took me by surprise. I had never known Adele Stein to speak this way about any resident—especially not one with as tragic a past as Dottie Luger.

"Today Dottie told me what happened to her family," I said. "It shook me up. In fact, it ruined my day. I feel sorry for her."

"She tells quite a story, doesn't she?" Adele Stein said. "You shouldn't believe her, though. She's lying."

"Lying? Why would she make something like that up?"

Adele Stein looked at me. Her eyes were rimmed with dark circles, and she looked sad and exhausted.

"Because Dottie's family is not the family that was murdered," Adele said. "Dottie never had children. Those were her neighbors."

"And the shock of their death made her think they were her own," I said, impressed with my own analysis of Dottie's mental state.

"More like a guilty conscience," Adele mumbled, absently fingering the Star of David that hung around her neck.

"What do you mean?" I asked.

Adele Stein hesitated. "Dottie Luger is not Jewish, even though she says she is. She's a Polish Catholic. Her neighbors were Jewish. She informed on them. She told the German authorities that she had a Jewish family living next door. The Germans came, shot the little girl and the mother on the doorstep. Then they burned the house with the father and boy in it. Dottie watched it all happen. It's *her* fault those people died."

It took me a few moments to find my voice. "How do you know? Did she tell you?"

"Mr. Ganz told me. He is also from Lodz. That's why he won't talk to her."

"Why does she insist on living in a Jewish home, then? She could go over to Nazareth Nursing Home and live among Catholics."

"She doesn't want to."

"Transfer her to a nursing home in South Buffalo," I suggested. "She'd be farther away, and she could speak Polish to everybody there."

"We tried that once. She took a bus and was back here in no time."

"Why don't you kick her out, then? Just tell her she can't be here anymore."

Adele sighed. "And where would she go? She can't be on her own. If she became a bag lady on Allen Street, I couldn't live with it."

Adele was lost in thought. Finally she said: "Maybe being here, among the Jews, is her way of repenting. It punishes her that the other residents despise her. She lives among the people whom she once betrayed, and tries to do good by taking care of Mrs. Shapira, as compensation for the evil she caused."

"Why can't everybody just forgive her, then?" I said. "She's sorry for what she did, and she is trying to make amends."

Adele looked at me with a level gaze. "The only people who have the power to forgive her are the ones she wronged. Even God cannot forgive a murderer on behalf of the victims. That, anyway, is how we Jews see it. I know you Catholics have a different view."

"But the people she wronged are dead. How can they forgive her?"

Adele Stein gave a slight shrug. "If there is an afterlife, maybe Dottie will have the chance to ask for forgiveness then."

"Dottie knows that her sins are forgiven through Jesus," I said, more to myself than to Adele Stein.

"If she believes that, then she ought to sleep well at night," Adele Stein said dryly.

Mrs. Levine shuddered, and then stopped breathing. Adele felt for a pulse, looked at her watch, then waited to see if she would revive. I sat there, certain that the spider's silk had been severed and that her soul was now on its journey upward.

Adele Stein again checked for Mrs. Levine's pulse, and said: "The time of death is twenty forty-four. Please write it on her chart. I'll call the family. Please tell Trina to call the funeral home."

THE
SYBARITE

IDIDN'T THINK I'D STAY at Restaurant Jean-Paul Galli as long as I have. It's been three years now. Everybody knows Jean-Paul is a genius. That's why his customers pay good money. Michelin wanted to give him stars, but he'd have none of it. So you won't find Restaurant Galli mentioned in their guide. Even so, his reputation is known all over the world. Despite his fame, he is the same disheveled kitchen dervish he was the day I met him. None of his success has gone to his head. He only cares about the food, not about the celebrity that so many chefs seem to crave these days. He won't even let people refer to him as "chef." "I am a cook," he insists, "nothing more."

Every night, all the tables in the restaurant are filled, and people must wait to get in. We are democratic here. Royalty, celebrities, politicians, and industrialists must wait, like everybody else.

The restaurant sits at the edge of a bluff overlooking the Mediterranean, on the outskirts of Nice. It looks Moorish, with arched windows and a recessed doorway. The white walls throw off a fierce glare in summer, a comforting orange glow in winter when the sun is low. The first time I saw the building, I almost passed by without a second look. But I was thirsty from walking along the stony beach, and I thought I might find a glass of water.

I would have preferred to make a selection from the menu posted next to the door, but it was the "help wanted" sign that caught my eye. I tried the door handle to see if it was locked. The heavy wooden door swung open on its hinges. It took several seconds for my eyes to adjust from the bright Mediterranean sun to the dim interior.

Stained-glass windows trapped the outside light, letting very little into the rest of the room. The low ceilings were divided by wooden beams. Oil paintings hung on the stone walls, created by some unknown artist who was obviously enamored of Van Gogh's *The Potato Eaters*.

And then there was the smell. There was the damp mustiness of a cellar (the cool stone walls exuded moisture), but there was also the heavenly aroma of garlic and herbs, olive oil and butter, and what else? I couldn't quite place it, but the rumbling in my stomach reminded me I hadn't eaten that day. I made my way to the back where I heard voices.

A woman came out of a doorway.

"Oh, hello," she said. "Come and sit down." She pulled out a chair from the wooden table. "You want a job, do you?"

I nodded. I knew I looked too shabby to be a customer. My backpack and sleeping bag were hidden behind a caper bush outside. I hoped I didn't look too desperate. I had only a few francs in my pocket, not enough for a good meal or decent lodging. I planned to camp on the beach after the sun went down.

"Let me tell Jean-Paul." She disappeared through the doorway and returned a moment later. "He will see you in just a few minutes," she announced.

She sat down across from me, and we studied each other. She was petite, with a mass of dark curly hair. Her eyes were deep black, like squid ink.

"You are French?" she asked after a few moments.

"French Canadian."

She smiled. "I'm from Italy myself. But I've lived in France since I was a teenager. Now it almost feels like home." She asked me a few more questions about my family and my previous employment. Before long, I was telling her about the death of my mother and my decision to come to Europe. I didn't tell her I had spent my pitifully small inheritance with reckless abandon in London and Amsterdam or that I planned to hitchhike my way to Tangier in a few weeks. She listened attentively to my story. Her face was sympathetic.

Sooner than I would have liked, our conversation was interrupted by a gruff voice from the kitchen.

"Marissa, send him in."

"Jean-Paul will see you now," she said, leading me into the next room.

The kitchen had only slightly more light than the dining room. A door opened into the side yard, letting in the sun, and an iron chandelier dangled from the dark-beamed ceiling. A few candles stuck in old teacups kept the shadows in the corners at bay. A lanky man scurried between a butcher block and the massive black stove, chopping, stirring, seasoning, tasting. Flames from big burners cradled the bottoms of copper pots and pans.

I watched him for several minutes before he looked up.

"Here, try this and tell me what you think." He shoved a plate at me.

I was hungry, but my appetite flagged when I saw what it was. There, neatly arranged in a circle of clarified butter, were six of the largest *escargots* I have ever seen. They were plump and meaty, their spiraled shells detached and balanced on each little morsel. A small bouquet of fresh herbs garnished the dish.

I hesitated.

"Well, go ahead," he said impatiently, and then he remembered to give me a fork.

I pushed aside a shell and speared one. It was delicious. I tried not to eat them all too quickly, but I was hungry, and they tasted better with each one I ate. I gave the plate back to him, empty.

"Well?" he demanded.

"Marvelous, and I don't even like escargots," I said.

He smiled, and then frowned. "The garlic. Does it overwhelm?"

"No, I don't think so," I said. "Although I do love garlic, so perhaps I am not the right one to ask."

He peered at me. "You speak French, but you are not from France. What are you?"

"Canadian."

"Which city?"

"Montreal."

"Ah," he said, nodding, "the Canadians from the big cities sometimes have a sophisticated palate. Give this same dish to a Swede or a Pole, and they'll complain that there is too much garlic. So I must find the balance."

He tipped a large wooden box to show me the contents. Inside were dozens of snails, happily feasting on herbs.

"I feed them only the best," he explained. "When they are big enough, I drown them in white wine. That way, the meat stays tender. They die trying to escape. No need to dig them out. It's a technique I invented."

My stomach turned at the sight of the slimy creatures whose brethren I just ate, but the lingering garlic-butter-herb taste in my mouth assuaged my guilt.

He looked me up and down. "I'll hire you to be one of my waiters, if my wife approves."

"I approve," Marissa called from the other room.

MANY CUSTOMERS DELUDE themselves into thinking that they're sophisticated gastronomes, but most of them wouldn't know good food from cattle feed. They come here to eat because everybody in their herd does it. They're more concerned with bragging to their friends about being seen here than they are in immersing themselves fully in the moment when they taste a creation from Jean-Paul.

But there are the few who come here for the food. Jean-Paul calls them the gastronomic aristocrats, and it is for them that he cooks. They are the ones who get that look in their eye when you bring the dish and set it in front of them. They do not care whether they are perceived as being in a chic place with other chic people. They are focused only on their food. And it has nothing to do with being rich or famous, because many of the gastronomic aristocrats are neither.

Many times Jean-Paul has chased me out of the kitchen when I told him that "His Highness So-and-so wishes to congratulate you on the chocolate biscuit in mandarin liqueur. And the dab of lavender ice cream, he says, is brilliant. He asks for you to come out so he may tell you in person how much he enjoyed his meal."

Jean-Paul waves me away, not bothering to look up. "You tell His Highness that I am in the middle of a delicate sauce, and I cannot come away from the stove." A pause. "My regrets," he adds, without regret.

But if I mention that there is a lone diner who has had his eyes closed for most of the meal, concentrating on each morsel, Jean-Paul turns his task over to the sous-chef, and slips into the dining room to have a few words with the unknown gourmand. Then Jean-Paul returns to the kitchen with a smile on his face, invigorated and inspired by the knowledge that for one evening, at least, his efforts have not gone unappreciated by a fellow member of the gastronomic aristocracy.

I DO NOT KNOW WHETHER my co-worker Dmitri considered himself a gourmand. He certainly had no patience with Jean-Paul's eccentric ways and made no secret of the fact that he considered our chef to be a self-absorbed dictator. Jean-Paul thought Dmitri insolent and probably would have fired him, except that Dmitri was the best waiter in the restaurant.

Dmitri seemed to care only for three things: money, cigarettes, and women. He had that nervous, restless energy of a heavy smoker who subsists on nicotine instead of food. He was always scrubbing his long fingers to remove the tar stains.

He used to slick back his dark hair with a citrus lotion to disguise the lingering smoke, but Jean-Paul put a stop to it.

"I cannot have all these other smells competing with my food," Jean-Paul announced at a staff meeting. "The customer's nose must be distracted by nothing except what I cook." We were thus all forbidden to wear perfume or shaving lotion of any kind. He would have forbidden his patrons to wear it, too, if he could have.

He despised Dmitri's smoking, and never allowed him to smoke on the job. During business hours, Dmitri resorted to chewing breath mints incessantly and drinking cold peppermint tea. After closing time, he'd sit at a table outside, a little way beyond the restaurant's kitchen door, overlooking the beach, and smoke cigarette after cigarette. He'd strum an old *balalaika*, a cigarette hanging from his thick lips, and brag about the women he'd seduced. He was my age, maybe a few years older, but I envied his worldliness and apparent ease with women. I thought he was Greek, but he told me he was really Macedonian. His French was almost as good as mine, with only a hint of an accent.

He always got the best tables, sold more bottles of wine than any of us, and knew exactly how to flatter customers without appearing obsequious or condescending.

One of his most successful strategies worked like this. A patron would order something from the menu, such as the filet mignon with sauce espagnole. Dmitri would first look over his shoulder, and then lean over and whisper conspiratorially: "That is usually an excellent choice, Madam, but tonight Jean-Paul is in rare form when it comes to his _____."

And then he would name a dish that was slightly less expensive, such as the sautéed pheasant breast with Madeira and grape sauce. The customers noticed this, and immediately trusted him all the more for his unselfish guidance. From there, it was easy to get them to order a more expensive wine to go with their meal, and perhaps a dessert or two.

For him, it was a game.

"After all," he told me once, "I have to work just as hard whether the bill comes to two thousand *francs* or three thousand francs. I'd rather work for the three thousand francs."

Dmitri would often tell his customers that he had that very day personally sampled whatever they had ordered, and he praised them for their discriminating taste. I wondered when he actually had tried these things, since I rarely saw him consume anything other than cigarettes, peppermints, and tea.

He had an uncanny sense of which customers were most likely to spend more, and he swooped down on their tables before any of us had a chance. He also monopolized the tables with the best-looking women. Some of the other waiters resented him for it, but I did not. He was arrogant and greedy—I'll be the first to admit that—but he was also entertaining and knowledgeable. I learned a lot from him and looked forward to our late-night conversations under the stars, drinking ouzo or pastis, listening to his tales and his balalaika.

He also had a devious, vengeful streak, as I learned soon after I met him. He told me about an incident at a hotel, where he had worked as a waiter in the restaurant.

"The pastry chef was French, from Paris. Lucien, that was his name," Dmitri said, fingering his balalaika. "Anyway, he knew I had been getting to know one of the waitresses, Odette. I was just a date or two from consummating our friendship, and Lucien swooped down and took her from right under my nose."

He strummed an angry, dissonant chord and continued. "Lucien was arrogant before, but now that he'd had her, he was completely unbearable. So one night after he had left, I slipped into the pantry and put milk powder in his cream of tartar. I shook it up and smelled it to be sure it was undetectable. Next day, he went to make meringues and sponge cakes. He had the bowl of egg whites, like this, ready to be beaten."

Dmitri put the balalaika on the table, and pretended it was the bowl. "In goes the cream of tartar. He beats and beats, and nothing happens! The whites won't expand because of the fat in the milk powder. He yells at the dishwasher, accusing him of not getting all the grease out of the mixing bowls. Then he throws the whole bowl of egg whites out the door." Dmitri laughed and lit another cigarette. "He cleans the bowl himself in hot water and detergent, and wipes it down with vinegar and salt. He separates three dozen more eggs. In goes the cream of tartar, and again, nothing! By this time, he is mad as a bull, because it is getting late and there are no fresh cakes yet. I had to hide my smile every time I came into the kitchen, because he was swearing up a storm, and I couldn't help but laugh. He got so far behind schedule on the baking, he almost lost his job. I don't know how many hours it took him to discover that the problem was in the cream of tartar. The fool."

Dmitri chuckled at his own cleverness, and resumed the soft strumming on the instrument, the cigarette hanging from his lips. I made a mental note to always stay on Dmitri's good side and never steal his tables—or his women.

One evening, Dmitri came up to me at the waiter's station and said: "You see that table over there?"

I had noticed the man with the beautiful woman when they walked in. Or more exactly, I had noticed the beautiful woman right away and then noted with dismay the presence of the man. She was exquisite: tall and blonde, with a figure that made every other woman in the restaurant look like a squat turnip. I knew Dmitri would be the one to wait on them. It was exactly the kind of table Dmitri always hoarded for himself.

"So?" I prompted him, expecting him to whet my appetite for some gossipy tidbit.

"The table is yours," he informed me.

"Why?"

"I'm too busy," he said, and abruptly turned away.

Too busy? Dmitri was never too busy to wait on a table of the very rich or the very beautiful. But I had no time to dwell on it. I immediately went over to take their order. They wanted a bottle of the best champagne in our cellar. I rushed to get it. I was so distracted by her, I almost forget how to open the champagne bottle without making a mess. And then the cork got stuck, and I struggled to get it free. I cursed myself for my clumsiness.

The man laughed good-naturedly. He tried to put me at ease by introducing himself.

"I am Michel Duval," he said in a lightly accented French, "and this is Kirsten Jenssen. We have heard so many good things about this fine restaurant."

The blonde woman focused her gorgeous blue eyes on me for an instant, and then turned her attention back to Michel Duval and said something in a language I didn't know.

"She does not speak French," Monsieur Duval explained. "But she does appreciate the finer things in life." His eyes sparkled, and he took her hand.

For the rest of the evening, they barely spoke another word to me. He kept his head bent so close to hers, their hair mingled. From the doorway of the kitchen, I watched with envy as he fed that gorgeous creature choice morsels from his plate, laughing quietly, holding her hand, and kissing her from time to time.

After the restaurant was closed, I told Dmitri about them.

"They were not shy about ordering," I reported. "Especially when it came to the champagne."

Dmitri didn't say anything.

"With the way their eyes were eating each other up, the food was probably a second-rate distraction," I said with a sly grin. "They were real gastronomes. He had the colbert of pork tenderloin, and didn't ask for more sauce, unlike many customers who smother their food with it. He even left an extra gratuity," I bragged, "just like an American. Only he isn't American."

Dmitri snickered. "No, he's not an American."

"Why didn't you take the table? They were your kind of customers."

"I told you: I was too busy."

The next time Michel Duval came to the restaurant, some weeks later, he had a different woman with him, but she was just as beautiful as the last. Her hair was the color of a new chestnut, and her red lips, in my estimation, would have made our finest Bordeaux taste like vinegar.

This time, I studied Michel Duval more carefully.

He was tall and broad-shouldered. His beard was trimmed to a point at his chin, and his almost-shoulder-length hair flowed in waves, like a lion's mane. It gave him an air of anachronistic elegance, as if he belonged in a more opulent era. He walked with the regal grace of a worldly man. It was only when I watched him make his way to the table that I noticed a slight limp in his gait.

I expected Dmitri to take their table this time, so I did not rush over until Dmitri said: "You're keeping your customers waiting."

"What?"

"The man over there with the woman," he pointed.

I rushed over and took their order. Again, throughout the evening, I watched them spend the next few hours nuzzling each other over the food. This time, I was a little less flustered by her beauty, but no less envious of him.

Later, Dmitri and I sat under the clear night sky, he strumming and smoking, me trying to make my glass of pastis last as long as possible.

"Michel Duval knows how to entertain a woman," I mused admiringly.

"Duval. So that's what he calls himself."

"Tell me, Dmitri, why don't you take their table? You could make good money and wait on the most beautiful woman in the place. That's always been your territory."

"I leave them to you. I shouldn't be too selfish, should I?"

"Did you suddenly develop a conscience or are you letting me in on your territory only to extract payment later?"

He shrugged. "I have my reasons." Before I could ask what they were, he launched into a folk song on his balalaika, pausing long enough to say: "Did I tell you about the time I met this raven-haired beauty in Budapest? It was in a small *konditorei* near the art gallery, where they served the best vanilla *kipferl* in Eastern Europe. She was the most exquisite thing...."

TWO MONTHS PASSED BEFORE I saw Michel Duval again. He smiled when I came to his table.

"How are you, Alain?" he asked warmly.

"Fine, thank you, Monsieur. Shall I bring out the champagne, or do you prefer to wait until your companion arrives?"

"Oh, there is no companion tonight. So please bring a glass of *eau minérale* while I decide."

"Very good, sir." I hid my disappointment that I wouldn't get to feast my eyes on his latest paramour.

I returned and set the *eau minérale* before him.

"I have a gift for Monsieur Galli," he said, giving me a heavy, tightly wrapped paper parcel. A rather repulsive odor clung to it. "A delicacy from Indonesia. Please tell him to unwrap it very carefully."

I took the parcel into the kitchen and deposited it on Jean-Paul's work counter, making sure to repeat Monsieur Duval's words of caution.

Jean-Paul was in the middle of assembling a pastry and paid no attention to me.

I waited on my other tables and came back into the kitchen in time to hear Jean-Paul complaining.

"What in the world is that smell?" he demanded.

I pointed to the parcel, and again repeated what Monsieur Duval had told me about unwrapping it.

Jean-Paul removed the paper, revealing a hideous ball covered with enormous spikes.

"Show me who brought it," he said.

I led him to Monsieur Duval's table.

"Thank you for the, er, gift," Jean-Paul began, "but I am not quite sure what you would like me to do with it."

"Why, the *durian* fruit is for your enjoyment," said Monsieur Duval. "I brought it back from Indonesia. It is my gift to you for all the wonderful meals I have had here. Of course, you know that it must be split open with a hatchet. Wielded by a practiced hand, if possible."

"Perhaps you would be good enough to show me," Jean-Paul suggested, always willing to learn a new thing and avoid hurting himself in the process.

He led Monsieur Duval to the kitchen and gave him a hatchet. Duval was undaunted by the murderous spikes, and in two or three deft strokes, he split the fruit open, revealing a creamy, pale-yellow interior. Monsieur Duval spooned some onto a plate and handed it to Jean-Paul.

"Amazing," the chef analyzed, his eyes closed. "Bananas … cream … and … ripe, flowing brie," he concluded.

He passed plates around for the rest of us. It was exactly as he described, and more. The flavor was complex and carnal.

Monsieur Duval must have read my thoughts. He said with a mischievous twinkle: "Like a woman, the durian is formidable and even impregnable on the outside, but creamy and yielding once you get past the forbidding exterior. The Indonesians believe it is an aphrodisiac."

"Truly remarkable to find this in a fruit," Jean-Paul declared. "A repellent odor, but a heavenly taste, like cheese. I am thinking of the possibilities …"

"Savor it now, because it is almost impossible to procure," said Monsieur Duval.

"Surely it is not *too* expensive?"

"Not particularly expensive, no, but banned from hotels and airplanes because of the odor. In this case, I was able to bring some back because I did not fly on a commercial airplane."

"Ah, I see," said Jean-Paul. "Well, perhaps you would like to sit awhile here in the kitchen. I am working on a new bouillabaisse, and I would like your opinion."

"Delighted," said Monsieur Duval.

"Did you try the durian?" I asked Dmitri at the waiter's station as we readied plates for the dining room.

"The what?"

"Durian. In the kitchen."

"I'll try it later."

I noticed that every time Dmitri came in the kitchen to get his orders, he avoided looking at Monsieur Duval. But Duval was too engrossed in his conversation with Jean-Paul to notice. He was also intensely interested in tasting the custom dishes being prepared for him. They were old friends by the end of the night. Monsieur Duval insisted on paying the bill, but Jean-Paul would have none of it.

"You were my guest, and I have been inspired because of our conversation," Jean-Paul said.

"Ah, but the pleasure was mine," Monsieur Duval returned.

Jean-Paul smiled, a rare thing for him.

"I will tell you what," said Monsieur Duval. "Next Thursday I will be here with a very special companion. Although she is wealthy, she is English and rather new to the world of food. I must initiate her slowly. But I will be ordering the best champagne you have in the house. The chanterelle ravioli and the acacia honey torte with wild berries ... well, they would be a perfect part of a perfect evening."

Jean-Paul held up his hands. "Say no more. I will have them, but *for you only*. They will not be on the menu. You remind Alain"—he pointed at me—"and they will appear."

The woman he brought a week later looked familiar. She was a celebrity, recently divorced from her royal husband, and very beautiful. Flaming red hair, scarlet lips. Her low-cut, emerald-green dress showed off her creamy white skin.

The meal was a success. Two nights later, Monsieur Duval stopped by at closing time to thank us.

"You were in rare form," he said to Jean-Paul. "She was enamored of everything put in front of her." He turned to me.

"And you, Alain, were the perfect waiter. She said her servants are clumsy oafs compared to you."

"And so it was a successful evening, then?" asked Jean-Paul, pleased.

"Too successful," said Monsieur Duval, chagrined. "We left here at about eleven o'clock, arrived at my place at around half past, and she proposed to me just before midnight. I had hardly even kissed her," he confessed. "But, naturally, I had to say no. I cannot get married."

No, of course not, I thought. It would be like asking him to dine only on osetra and foie gras every night for the rest of his life.

MONTHS PASSED, and the brilliant, sun-washed days of August were upon us. The restaurant was closed for three weeks while Jean-Paul and his wife took a vacation in Italy. I stayed in Nice. I had gotten used to it; it was the closest thing to a home I had. Also, I was too heavy-hearted to travel.

There had been girlfriends over the years, but the latest one, Claudine, was as close to perfect as I had come in a long time. After two weeks of dating, she informed me that she wanted to be "just friends." After a stormy break-up on the phone, I left my flat and installed myself at my favorite small café, sulking and nursing a glass of pastis. I tried to derive some solace by reading St. Exupéry's *Le Petit Prince*. But I was restless and unhappy.

"You look like you could use a good night on the town, with plenty of ministrations from the fairer sex," said Dmitri.

He dragged a heavy duffel bag next to the table and took the seat across from me.

"I've had enough of women for now," I said. "They're nothing but heartache and trouble." I pointed to the bag. "Are you going on vacation?"

"Yeah." Dmitri motioned the waiter for a drink and pulled out a cigarette. "Enough of women, eh? Tsk, tsk. What would your hero Monsieur Duval think if he heard you talking like that?"

"He would laugh, I'm sure. He doesn't let petty things like love get in the way of his own happiness. If only I had his talent for picking the prettiest peach on the tree, I wouldn't mind those times when my basket is empty. He is one of the luckiest men alive. I wish I were more like him."

Dmitri looked at me with a dead-serious expression. "There is a proverb: 'Be careful what you wish for, or you may get it.'"

"What could be wrong with wishing to be extremely handsome, extremely rich, and extremely popular with the most beautiful women in the world? I'd trade places with him in a minute, and never regret it." I laughed, but I meant every word.

Dmitri did not laugh. He leaned forward and spoke with an intensity that I'd never seen in him before. "Don't tempt Fate like that! You are so ignorant. Have you ever seen the fat old countess who comes in and smacks her lips over the mountain oysters? Do you think she gives a thought to the poor beast who lost them for her gustatory pleasure? No. She does not. And Fate will feast on you with the same pitiless *goût* if you are not careful."

"You ascribe too much power to Fate. We are, after all, beings with free will." I braced myself for an intellectual argument, and hoped my knowledge of philosophy wasn't too stale.

He grunted and waved away my comment. "Free will has nothing to do with it. I am talking about accidents."

"What has that to do with Monsieur Duval? I suppose you'll say it's an accident that he's so rich and so attractive to all the beautiful women."

"Things are not always what they appear."

I thought a moment. "Oh. Don't tell me. Monsieur Duval really prefers to make love to men, right?" I said sarcastically.

"If only he could."

"What do you mean?"

Dmitri looked at me, deliberating whether he should go on. He stubbed out the cigarette and lit another one. "Oh, I suppose it doesn't matter. I'm leaving for good. I gave my notice a few weeks ago. Jean-Paul is happy to be rid of me. Now you'll be the headwaiter. You'll make all the money."

"Where are you going?"

"Home. To Rostov."

"Rostov? I thought you were Macedonian."

"My father is. But home is Russia, and that's where I'm headed."

I paused a few moments to digest all this news. "So what about Duval?" I prodded him, turning back to the subject that interested me more than Dmitri's plans to go home. "You were going to tell me about him."

"You've been so awestruck with the man, thinking he's as virile as a lion, with his gorgeous women. The fact is, kissing is about as far as he can get."

"What do you mean?"

"He's physically incapable of making love to a woman. He's got nothing down there, understand? So he seduces women with food. That's all he can do." Dmitri blew smoke out of his nose, and for a moment the plumes curled around his upper lip like a big moustache, and then quickly dissolved.

Then he chuckled mirthlessly. "His real name is Mikhail Diaghilev. A distant relative of the ballet impresario. We were in the Russian Army together. Or rather, I was just a low-ranking soldier and he was a commanding officer, competent and good to his men. But his weakness, if you could call it that, was his love of all the finest things in life. Wine, food, women, art—everything was luxury with him. His office, a dim little room in a barracks, had real Persian rugs and gold-framed paintings on the walls. We used to call him the Sybarite."

"Sybarite?"

"After the ancient city of Sybaris. Legend has it that the inhabitants of Sybaris were fabulously wealthy and loved pleasure more than anything."

Dmitri paused to drink, and remained silent for a while.

"Well, what happened?" I prodded.

"You ever been a soldier?"

"No."

"Then let me tell you something. Soldiers are supposed to be Spartan. That's what makes them tough. Love of luxury makes one appear too soft, too aristocratic. And aristocrats, along with the rich and successful, are not popular in Russia. That was Diaghilev's problem."

He looked out at passers-by and sipped his drink absentmindedly.

"So he wasn't popular?" I said.

"He was, he was," Dmitri said, nodding emphatically. "He could be very tough, and decisive. He was a good politician, an excellent commander. He inspired loyalty. Of course, he had many enemies. He was especially popular with women, and naturally, even his friends envied him this."

I was impatient to hear the rest. "So how did he, uh, get to where he is today?"

Dmitri held up his hand. "I'm getting to that. First, I need a refill."

He motioned the waiter, and he wouldn't resume his story until more pastis arrived.

Finally, he spoke. "My unit was assigned to put down rebels on the border. They called it routine, but there was nothing routine about it. It was war, pure and simple, no matter what they told us. Soldiers died there, and we all knew our lives were at stake, even on the supposedly safe patrols. Diaghilev was already there with other top commanders, designing strategies. I remember the day I heard about his accident. I was with four or five other soldiers in a tavern, and we were flirting with some of the local girls. One of our comrades came running in the place and said: 'Did you hear what happened to Diaghilev?'

"'He finally laid General Borov's wife!' one of us joked. We all laughed.

"The messenger didn't smile. 'No,' he said. 'He was in a bad accident. Land mine. Blew his nuts right off. They think he'll make it, but he can kiss his sex life goodbye.'

"We were all shaken and we didn't talk for a few minutes. The girls slipped away because we were no fun anymore. We went back to our bunks with our own thoughts. Here was a man who stood for all we secretly wanted to be, at least as far as women were concerned, and in one afternoon, he was cooked. I told myself that if it were me, I'd toss off a bottle of vodka and put a bullet in my brain."

Dmitri finished the rest of his drink in one gulp, and put down his glass.

"We knew the countryside was full of land mines. That's what got him. Then rumors started that the explosion was no accident. Someone suggested a cuckolded husband's revenge; others said it was a woman whose advances he had refused; still others suggested a political rival. But it didn't matter, did it? The end result was the same."

"So that's why you avoided him at the restaurant?"

Dmitri nodded. "I hope he didn't recognize me. I don't think he did. He wouldn't want to be reminded of it any more than I, although he's the one who has to live with it every day." He got a pensive look on his face. "He is a brave one, though. Looking at him you'd never guess that Fate has feasted on him. He lives as if he has outwitted Fate." He crushed out his cigarette and pushed the ashtray away.

"Is that why he had a different woman all the time? Because they found out what he lacked, and let him go?" I asked.

Dmitri shrugged. "Perhaps *he* let them go before they ever discovered it."

He looked at his watch, and stood up. "My train leaves soon. Take care and good luck." He held out his hand, and we shook. I watched him disappear down the street, lugging his duffel bag over his shoulder.

Several months passed before I saw Monsieur Duval again. One Thursday night in December, he came in alone, looking tan, well rested, and splendidly dressed.

"Ah, Alain, my friend," he said when I came up to his table. "How are you? I have missed this place," he said, looking around and breathing in the heavenly aromas.

"It is good to see you, sir," I responded. "You have been away?"

"I have just come back from Athens, and I am expecting my dinner companion any time now."

He motioned for me to come closer.

"Her name is Mademoiselle Celeste," he confided. "They found her homeless and unconscious after her village had been bombed and raided by enemy soldiers. She was almost dead from starvation."

I thought about what Dmitri had told me.

Duval saw me shudder and interpreted it as concern for his companion.

"Oh, do not worry about her," he said. "Some good nuns took her in until she regained her strength. I met her at the home of an old friend, an embassy official in Athens whose sister is a nun at the convent. The nun thought the girl might be a good tutor for my friend's children. Mademoiselle Celeste knows music and at least three languages. She is very intelligent, and a saint besides. I was captivated by her, and you will be too. I insisted that she take a short holiday and come here to France. I promised to get her back to Athens in time for Christmas. She is a devout Christian, you know."

"And is her health improved?" I asked.

"Oh yes. Now she is much better. But we must go gently with her. No meat. Only fish and vegetables. She is austere when it comes to food. Plain boiled rice and beans were her sustenance for a long time. Anything more exotic than that, and … well, we must give it time." He chuckled gently.

"If I may make a suggestion, then. The cream of celeriac soup is particularly mild. And the broiled flounder fillet is very fresh."

"That sounds perfect," said Monsieur Duval. "And perhaps we can persuade her to try something a little more decadent for dessert. I believe she likes chocolate."

His gaze turned to someone in the doorway and his face lit up. "Ah, here she is."

Marissa guided Celeste to Duval's table. Celeste was draped in a sky-blue, ankle-length dress with long sleeves. A sky-blue veil covered her head and shoulders. She lowered it, revealing a splendid head of dark hair arranged in a twisted plait that gave the vague impression of a halo. She was a fragile, unblemished waif, so different from the worldly, voluptuous women with whom he usually shared his table.

The two spoke quietly. He explained each dish as I presented it, and took great pleasure watching her eat. He did not even touch her. But the gentle, protective tenderness with which he gazed at her told me that here was a man who, if not in love at that moment, was certainly sliding in that direction.

After dinner, she excused herself from the table and glided toward the powder room.

Monsieur Duval watched her with unabashed admiration and then motioned me over.

"I think she likes everything," he said. "It won't be long until she's ready for the superb escargots and the roast veal. But tonight, chocolate will be rushing things. She needs something more suitable for an innocent palate. Perhaps a *crème bruleé* with a few raspberries. Explain it to Jean-Paul, will you? He will understand."

9

THE RIVER'S END

THE MOTHER AND DAUGHTER sat on a wooden bench in their front yard, shucking corn. The trees were still summer green, but here and there red and yellow leaves glowed among the branches.

"Does she have to stay here for good?" the girl whined.

"Shh, lower your voice, Missy. She might hear you," Theresa whispered. "Granny has nowhere to go. She can't take care of herself anymore."

"But, Mom, she's driving me crazy!" Missy pulled the husks off the corn with an impetuous jerk. Silky yellow threads floated down, tickling her knees. She brushed them away. "She always calls me 'girl.' I'm thirteen already. I'm not a girl. It gets on my nerves."

"She doesn't mean any harm by it. She used to call me 'girl' when I was younger." Theresa couldn't remember whether it had bothered her. She didn't think it had.

"And then she's always telling me about the old days. About our heritage, and how important it is."

"Well, our heritage *is* important," Theresa observed. "One day you'll appreciate Granny's stories. You should listen to her while you still have the chance."

Missy rolled her eyes. "She's so annoying. I wish she'd just go away already."

Theresa lost her patience. "She's not going anywhere. She can't even walk. If it makes her happy to talk, we can have the courtesy to listen. Deal with it, okay?" Theresa was tired of these discussions. Granny had come to live with them two weeks ago, and Missy seemed to have a new complaint every day. Well, school would be starting soon. Then Missy would have other things to distract her.

Missy finished shucking the corn in silence. "I'm going to the river, Mom. I'll be back soon."

"Don't be late for dinner," Theresa called after her. "Be back in an hour."

Missy rode her bicycle out of their small gravel driveway, made a few short turns and was soon riding along the road, following the course of the river. She pedaled half a mile to her favorite spot: a small grove of trees hiding the remains of a dock that jutted out into the water.

She sat on the dock and threw stones. Her tan, long legs dangled over the edge, the tips of her sneakers making gentle ripples on the surface the water. The sun was setting, casting a shimmering gold veneer over everything. Out in the middle of the river, the golden light camouflaged the current, making the river look languid, almost still.

She wasn't fooled by its peaceful appearance. That current had almost taken her life last summer.

It happened when she hadn't been paying attention—a stupid mistake for someone who grew up there. She got overconfident, went out a little too far, and before she knew it, the swift fingers of the Niagara River plucked her into the current and carried her downstream as effortlessly as if she were a small twig. It had taken all her strength to swim back to the shore. She'd had several miles to go before she would have seen the mist of Niagara Falls, but the certainty of where the river was taking her filled her with terror. The falls had claimed many lives: some were suicides, but most were daredevils who thought they could brave the 158-foot drop over the falls clad only in a barrel or some other homemade contraption. It wasn't the descent that got them, but the enormous boulders at the bottom, hidden by the thick walls of cascading water and roiling waves. A human body had no chance against them. It would be shattered by the fall, and then crushed and drowned by the tons of water that came crashing down on those rocks every second.

She'd never told anyone about the incident, not even her mother. But she did have nightmares every so often. It was always the same dream: She was swimming in safe water, when suddenly she was swept toward the precipice of the falls, powerless to stop. The roar of the water drowned her screams. She always managed to wake up, shaking with fear, just as she was about to go over.

"GET ME THE CORN HUSKS, will you, girl?" Granny said after dinner that night. "I want to show you something."

"But we threw them out," Missy protested.

"That's okay," Granny said. "Be a good girl and get them out of the trash bin, won't you? They won't be hard to find."

Missy sighed and went outside. She dug around in the trash can, searching for the paper bag with the discarded husks. She would have complained to her mother, but Theresa was out working the evening shift. Then she remembered her mother's words: *Deal with it.*

Missy went back into the house. She put the bag on the table in front of her grandmother.

"Sit down, girl," Granny said.

Missy did as she was told and sat across from the old woman, crossed her arms, and pouted.

Granny's legs were weak, but her hands and arms were strong. She ripped open the bag, flattened it, and arranged the husks neatly in front of her, piling the silky yellow threads to the side. Her eyes glittered keenly as she worked, and her mouth was set in a firm, determined line. Her white hair, braided and twisted into a bun at the nape of her neck, was as thick as a young woman's.

"I'm going to show you how to make a cornhusk doll," Granny announced. "This way, you'll have something to show your kids when you're older. Something from your heritage."

Missy suppressed a groan and hoped Granny didn't see her roll her eyes.

"Fetch me some cotton and some thread, girl," Granny ordered. When Missy returned, Granny said, "Now look at how I do this. I use some cotton for the head." She wrapped a long cornhusk over the cotton, and tied it off with thread. "And more cotton for the chest. You try it."

Missy reluctantly obeyed. In a few minutes, she found she was enjoying it, or at least not minding it too much.

The old woman's face softened into a wistful smile, full of memories. "When I was a girl, we didn't have money for toys. We used what was around. I'd string tiny flowers on threads and use them as necklaces for the doll."

They worked in silence for a while, shaping the green, pliable husks into little figures. Missy let her mind wander, wondering what teachers she'd get when she returned to school, whether she'd be in the same class as her best friend Anna.

"I'm going to die soon, you know," Granny said calmly, as if she were commenting on the weather.

Missy jerked her head up, startled out of her own thoughts. "Don't say that!"

"It's true. I know my time is coming. And I know it'll be easier on you and your mother when I'm not around to bother you anymore. It won't be too much longer."

Missy tried to think of something to say. "You're healthy. You have many more years left, I'm sure."

Granny chuckled dryly. "My legs are no good. It's just a matter of time before the rest of me goes."

"But aren't you scared?" Missy didn't mean to ask, but it slipped out before she stopped herself.

Granny kept her gaze focused on her work. "No, my girl, I'm not scared. Look around you. The trees, sky, earth, water. I will become a part of them, part of God's creation…." She paused. "If I thought you could get away with it, I'd have you and your mother give me a river burial, right above the falls. I've always wanted to know what it was like to be in that powerful water." She smiled as one would smile at the prospect of taking a particularly enjoyable adventure.

"You'd want us to put you over the falls? When you're dead?" Missy asked, incredulous.

"If I could have my way. But you'd get in a lot of trouble if you tried it. So, I think a traditional burial in the ground is good enough. At that cemetery down the road. The one that overlooks the river." Granny held up her cornhusk doll, perfectly shaped and topped with corn silk hair. "There. Now it needs to dry for a few weeks."

"I'm afraid of the falls. In my dreams, I mean," Missy blurted, surprised that she had allowed herself to reveal her secret. But she couldn't stop. "I almost drowned in the river last summer. I swam too far out, and the current got me. I was headed for the falls. I almost didn't make it to shore, and then I had to walk home. It took me all afternoon to get back." It felt good to tell someone about it.

"So now the river has a special meaning for you," Granny said with a knowing smile.

"I guess you could say that," Missy said thoughtfully. "But I don't see why I still dream about it. It happened last summer. It's over."

"Our fears and dreams come from the same place. The dreams try to tell you something, you know."

"What are they saying, my fears and my dreams?" Missy was eager to have somebody tell her the secrets of her own heart.

The old woman shrugged. "Your fears and dreams belong to you. Only you can find out what they mean. Nobody can tell you. But in time, you will understand."

WHEN SCHOOL STARTED, Missy was surprised that she actually looked forward to her time with Granny. She'd come home to find that Granny had made her a cup of tea and a snack. Missy would sit at the kitchen table and talk to Granny, relating her progress in her classes and the latest gossip among her friends. Every few days, Granny showed her how to make something new out of things around the house. Old scraps of leather were sewn to make pouches for spare change, broken jewelry was restrung into beaded necklaces, sugar and nuts were boiled into candy, remnants of fabric were pieced together to make tiny quilt squares that would be fashioned into pot-holders or a bigger quilt. Maybe when the weather got a little colder, she and Granny could build a fire in the yard to roast apples and fish, just as her great-great-grandparents had. And in the winter, they could boil maple syrup, and then cool it by dribbling it into the fresh snow to make lacy hard-candy wafers. Her friends would be impressed.

ONE FRIDAY AFTERNOON in October, the air was crisp and full of sun and autumn colors. On her way home from school, Missy started to plan her weekend. She'd buy some beads from the store, then ask Granny to help her make a few more necklaces so she could give them to her friends at school on Monday.

When she turned the corner on her street, her eagerness turned to dread. An ambulance was in the driveway.

Her mother and two paramedics crowded the tiny bedroom. Granny was in bed, feebly waving away the strangers.

"I won't leave this house," she said, her voice raspy and weak.

The paramedics looked at Theresa. "We can't force her to go if she doesn't want to," one of them said.

Missy squeezed her way past them to her grandmother's side. "What happened? What's going on?" she cried, grasping her grandmother's hand.

Granny smiled. "It's time, girl. They want to take me to the hospital, but I want to die here. It's no use sticking me with needles."

Missy's mother was quietly weeping. The paramedics waited. Missy clutched her grandmother's hand tighter. The skin was papery, like an old cornhusk.

"Well, then, you won't go," Missy insisted, her voice shrill and loud. "I won't let them take you out of here."

The old woman closed her eyes. Her breathing was loud and labored. "Open the window, girl. I need fresh air." Missy leaped up to do as she was told. The paramedics left the room and waited near the front door. Theresa followed them, unable to watch her mother get weaker.

"If I could, I'd have you take me outside and put me among those beautiful trees so I could slip off quietly," Granny whispered. "But I think it would distress your mother too much. So, we'll keep the window open instead."

Missy had an idea. "I'll be right back. Please, Granny, wait until I get back." She darted outside, past her mother and the paramedics, who were discussing in hushed voices what should be done next.

"What are you doing?" Theresa asked, watching the girl scoop up handfuls of red, orange, and yellow leaves into a basket. Missy was too intent on her task to hear her. She cut a few graceful branches off the weeping willow, along with whatever late-blooming flowers she could find.

Granny appeared to be sleeping. Missy put flowers and leaves around the old woman on the pillow and blanket and carefully arranged some in her white hair. She tucked a small bouquet of yellow flowers and colored leaves in the wrinkled hands. She put the remainder on the table next to the bed so Granny could see them when she woke up. The sweet, earthy odor of the autumn foliage filled the room. Granny's eyes flickered open for an instant and then closed. "Thank you, my dear," she whispered. "It's almost as good as being outside. I have to go now. Don't be afraid. It's the way of things."

Missy held her grandmother's hand, and watched to see whether the old woman's chest was still rising and falling with each breath. She imagined it did long after it had stopped.

THE DREAM WAS DIFFERENT this time. Missy stood on the shore and watched her grandmother go over the falls.

What was the dream saying to her now?

She woke up and tried to think about things in a new way. She started with the day she almost perished in the terrifying current of the river. Then she thought about Granny. The pain of losing her was worse now, even though it had been a week since the funeral.

Missy rode her bicycle up the road, keeping pace with the river's swift current that ran parallel to her.

There were a few tourists taking pictures against the watery backdrop where the river fans out and becomes the half-mile horseshoe-shaped expanse of Niagara Falls. Missy walked her bicycle to the railing and leaned over to see the massive waterfalls. A fine mist prickled her face and hands. She enjoyed the sensation, even though it was chilly and made her shiver.

The noise of the falls vibrated in her head and chest, like a million drums and chanting voices. Every sound water could make was made here, from the lowest rumble vibrating through the rock precipice to the highest-pitched splash. It was a cacophony of rushing water, and all other sounds were drowned in it.

Missy walked to her favorite spot nearest the crest. There, the water was rippled and choppy, getting ready to fall over the edge. When the light was right, the water was a deep, transparent green, almost emerald. The rocky ledge over which the water flowed was just a foot or two below the water's surface, perfectly visible through the rippling green water. A mere body length later, the deep green fell away and became the white wall of crashing water known as Niagara Falls.

The tourists were gone. Missy was alone.

She reached into her jacket pocket. The cornhusk dolls had turned from a pliable bright green to a brittle yellow-brown. Granny's doll was more perfect, but hers wasn't too bad. She looked at them, remembering the good times when they'd been created. She wiped her tears away with the back of her hand. Then she threw the dolls over the railing. They landed exactly where she had hoped, in the deep green at the river's end. In a breath, they were swept over the edge, down into the falls, to become one with the water.

The End

ABOUT THE AUTHOR

CHRISTINE SILK earned her B.A. in English (cum laude) at Binghamton University, and a M.A. and Ph.D. in Rhetoric from Carnegie Mellon University. She has taught courses on writing, communication theory, literary analysis, and political philosophy. Christine lives in Southern California with her husband and children. Visit her website and blog at *ChristineSilk.com*. You can also connect on Facebook.

Afterword

THIS BOOK COULD NOT have happened without the help of many people. Thank you to the Literati Cafe writer's group for all the comments and suggestions when these stories were in rougher shape. You know who you are: Richard G., Andy G., Elite B., Dennis O., and especially Jennifer Bosworth, an excellent writer who has remained a thoughtful critic and friend through the years.

I am grateful to those teachers who pushed me to become a better writer, including Richard Young, Joseph Shanahan, and Esther Gardner. Thank you to those who have read drafts of these stories, and offered valuable insights, including Fernanda Hurwitz, Shaili Jain, and Stephen Marmer. I am grateful to I. Harry David for his help. Special gratitude goes to the team at 1106 Design. A special thank-you to my mother, Dolores Murphy, whose patient guidance turned me into an avid reader, and my father, Joseph Patrick Murphy (1940–2008), whose love of good stories rubbed off on me. Thank you to my sister, Kelly, whose plucky boldness was one of the inspirations for how I shaped the character of Lisa Gonzalez in "Chase the Sun." Another special thank-you goes to my brother Joe Muphy of *Ingenious.org*, who created my website, *ChristineSilk.com*, and who has been more than generous with technical advice.

Finally, many thanks and much love to my husband and to my children for their endless support and enthusiasm. I love you all more than I can say.

Christine Silk
Los Angeles, California
October 2015

Made in United States
North Haven, CT
26 February 2023

33174759R00125